My darling Cousin Addi,

I know you think I am being extremely inconvenient with all of this high drama. Sprinkling my ashes on blue stones and reading letters after you do it. But there is a reason.

You are the only person in the entire world, who I trust to do this.

You are the only person who would even countenance what I am about to say. Only the people with a distinct T in the lines of their palms can do it. You have that T, Addi. Most people have five main lines in their hands you have two.

Just two.

It is obvious that you are different.

It is obvious that you are one of them.

NEVER TOO LATE

BRENDA BARRETT

JAMAICA
TREASURES

Never Too Late
A Jamaica Treasures Book/January 2017

Published by Jamaica Treasures
Kingston, Jamaica

This is a work of fiction. Names, characters, places, and incidents are either the product of the author's imagination or are used fictitiously. Any resemblance to an actual person or persons, living or dead, events, or locales is entirely coincidental.

978-976-8247-50-6
Jamaica Treasures
P.O. Box 482
Kingston 19
Jamaica W.I.
www.fiwibooks.com

ALSO BY BRENDA BARRETT

FULL CIRCLE
NEW BEGINNINGS
THE PREACHER AND THE PROSTITUTE
AFTER THE END
THE EMPTY HAMMOCK
THE PULL OF FREEDOM
REBOUND SERIES
THREE RIVERS SERIES
NEW SONG SERIES
BANCROFT SERIES
MAGNOLIA SISTERS SERIES
SCARLETT SERIES
WILEY BROTHERS SERIES

ABOUT THE AUTHOR

Books have always been a big part of life for Jamaican born Brenda Barrett, she reports that she gets withdrawal symptoms if she does not consume at least two books per week. That is all she can manage these days, as her days are filled with writing, a natural progression from her love of reading. Currently, Brenda has several novels on the market, she writes predominantly in the historical fiction, Christian fiction, comedy and romance genres.

Apart from writing fictional books, Brenda writes for her blogs blackhair101.com; where she gives hair care tips and fiwibooks.com, where she shares about her writing life.

You can connect with Brenda online at:
Brenda-Barrett.com
Twitter.com/AuthorWriterBB
Facebook.com/AuthorBrendaBarrett

Chapter One

"**A**re you sure about this, Addi?" Josh asked her concerned.

"Yes, I am sure." Addi barely managed to restrain herself from snapping at her brother who was looking at her and the urn she clutched in her arms skeptically, as if he thought she had finally lost it. She had just settled down in the car and told him her reason for her impromptu visit to Jamaica.

"Sky told you to scatter her ashes by the blue rock in the old yard in Mandeville?" Josh was speaking as if she had a hearing impairment.

"Yes." Addi nodded vigorously. Josh looked slightly annoyed. She had called him only this morning to pick her up from the airport. He had sounded quite happy to do it at the time. He probably thought that she was going to be staying with him for a holiday and not for this quest that she had decided to honor for Sky's sake.

"How will she know that you did it?" Josh pulled out of the Norman Manley airport parking lot. "You could throw it in that flower bed, and she wouldn't know. It wouldn't matter. It's just ashes."

Addi glanced at the digital clock. It was ten fifty-nine. The morning sunlight was weak; she hoped it didn't rain today.

She tried to change the subject because she didn't want to have to defend herself for doing what Sky asked.

"You look haggard," she muttered. Her brother had gained weight, mostly around his midsection, and his face looked puffy, and there were large bags under his eyes. They were rimmed with a generous dark smudge as if he had not been sleeping.

Despite this, he was still handsome, with his narrow straight face and exotically slanted eyes. It was just that today he was looking more like a street hobo than Tyson Beckford.

Josh glanced at her. "You don't look so hot yourself. You are not sleeping, are you?"

"It's been a tough couple of weeks," Addi sighed. The beige t-shirt and khaki pants she was wearing did not add a hint of color to her person.

She looked out the window and caught her reflection in the rear-view mirror. She looked every day of her thirty-nine years and then some.

Her hair was in a finger wave style, which had felt like a great idea at the time, she had gotten quite good at it since she had chopped off her hair a few weeks ago in a fit of liberation. It had been stringy and unhealthy looking anyway.

Her makeup was troweled on and applied without her usual care because she had been on a hurry and wanted to hide her sleepless start, but she couldn't entirely hide the ravages of the last couple of days.

She dragged her eyes from her reflection and out at the

scenery.

It always gave her a special buzz when she arrived on Jamaican soil. Today that buzz was missing, maybe because it was shaping up to be a gray day and her mission in the country was a sad one.

Josh looked at the urn pointedly again. He wasn't going to give up the subject so quickly.

"I'll stop so you can scatter her ashes over the sea wall."

"I have to go." Addi blinked her eyes rapidly. "She asked me to in her will."

"Why should you carry out her will when she committed suicide? Obviously, her will was warped!" Josh snorted.

"Josh, please stop!"

Josh glanced at the tears at the corners of her eyes and then back to the road again. "It was a very selfish thing to do and so unlike Sky. She had so much to live for. She was happy, wasn't she? She told me she had just met this guy from the Middle East and she lived in that gigantic apartment in New York. When I visited last year, I was blown away by how rich she was. She had a good job, chief executive officer of a huge company."

Addi could again feel the pressing weight of grief as Josh listed all of Sky's material accomplishments. He was right. Sky had lived the kind of life that a vast number of people could only dream about.

Addi cleared her throat before speaking. "But I don't think Sky was ever happy. I mean, not since Rusty."

"Rusty Brown?" Josh glanced at her. "You serious? Crusty Rusty? The construction guy? The one who killed Uncle Stan?"

"Yes, him. They had a thing. Sky once told me that she would never love anybody the way she loved him."

Josh shook his head. "That's so, melodramatic! Crazy!

Unheard of! Why would she love the guy who killed her father and how would she even know what love is, she was just, what, fifteen years old?"

"About that age, yes." Addi inhaled raggedly. "But every time we saw each other, and I do mean every single Sunday for the past ten years, all my conversations with Sky included some snippet about Rusty Brown. No matter which guy she was seeing, he could be rich, he could be drop dead gorgeous, he could be sweet, he could be all three of those things combined...every single time, it was Rusty. I think that was her greatest regret."

Addi closed her eyes and swallowed. "We all have regrets. Don't you have any?"

Josh snorted. "Oh yes, thanks for asking. I am a bag of regrets. My whole life up to now has been one big glorious regret."

Addi shifted in her seat. "I know there are some obvious stuff, but what makes you say that?"

"Well for one, I regret not taking that MIT scholarship."

"Oh yeah, you wanted to do something in computers, huh?"

"Yep." Josh nodded. "I was in second year of college here when I got the scholarship. Boy, I loved programming. I could have been the next dot-com something or built some world-changing program or something. Who knows?"

He sighed dramatically. "But then Ellie got pregnant, and then we got married, and by that January the scholarship offer had expired. She had such a difficult pregnancy. It was so bad I had to stay home with her."

Addi nodded. "I remember." She inhaled sorrowfully. "I found Dad on the back step crying after it happened."

"Seriously?" Josh shrugged, "I have never believed that story. Dad has never said a word to me about it."

"I think he was more disappointed than you were." Addi

smiled sadly. "Parents are weird creatures. Sometimes they hide their disappointments because they don't want you to feel bad."

"They didn't hide their disappointment when I found out that Nelson wasn't mine after he became sick and our blood types were not compatible." Josh snorted, "And they didn't even bother to pretend that they were anything but angry when they had to pay for the divorce.

"It was all my fault. All of it, I threw away my future for some other man's kid. Up to this day, Ellie won't say who she was sleeping with before she decided to pin Nelson on me."

Addi sighed. "How is Nelson these days?"

"Rehab, last I heard. Prescription meds." Josh grimaced. "I keep tabs on him because, for the first three years of his life, I thought he was mine."

"And Ellie? Where is she now?" Addi looked at her brother in compassion; he had really had it rough with Ellie. She had wrung him out to dry. Their parents had feared for his sanity after the Ellie episode. His world had collapsed when he found out that Nelson wasn't his son.

"She is around." Josh snorted, "still looks good. She has a cooking show on one of the cable channels. I sometimes wish that she would age like an old hag, but every time I see her, she looks better. And I still feel..."

He stopped and inhaled. "I still feel for her Addi...it's ridiculous. It's like the anger cooled and the attraction kicks in, but I can't forget that she is like a dangerous snake. Pretty to look at but leaves a poisonous bite."

Addi sighed.

"Seriously, though," Josh muttered, "I wish I had nothing to do with her in the first place. I wish I never met her. She is the reason why my life is like this. I teach students at a community college whose only interest in computers is how to find the best porn sites. I am wasted there, but I have to do it. And to make matters worse, I don't entirely trust my current wife the way I should, and I secretly did DNA tests on Ken and Nancy just to be sure that they were mine.

"And to be brutally honest I have never been quite happy either. I should have met Avery first or not met Ellie at all."

Addi glanced at Josh; he was in the throes of some very unpleasant memories. His fingers gripped the steering wheel tightly, and a vein throbbed at the side of his head.

"Avery is a wonderful woman, Josh. I thought that you were completely and totally happy now. When Mom calls, she harasses me about how happy and well-adjusted you are. At least one of her children got it right."

"What does anybody know about what really goes on in other people's heads?" Josh shrugged. "I thought Sky was happy. Hell, I even thought you were happy, living the single life, lecturing at New York University with the big doctor in front of your name and all."

Addi shrugged. "I am okay..."

"But, not happy." Josh turned on the highway and picked up speed. "I mean generally. God knows these past couple of weeks were not for laughs. You are not going to do a Sky thing on me, are you? Because let me tell you now, you would totally ruin me."

Addi smiled tremulously. "No, I am not going to do a Sky thing on you, at least not so close to my birthday. Can you believe that I am going to be forty years old tomorrow?"

"Unbelievable, it seemed like just the other day the parents brought you home and declared that I had a new baby sister." Josh grinned and patted her knee. "A part of life is getting older Sis. Embrace it."

Addi smirked. "I do embrace it. I just wish..."

"You had Sky here to celebrate it with?" Josh sighed, "you

would think that she would live for you at least. You two were so close."

"Yes." Addi sighed. "I blame myself a little about that. I had no idea that she would..."

"I know." Josh nodded. "I don't think anybody in the family can say they feel blameless. We are all asking ourselves, why. Was Aunt Ivy at the funeral?"

"Yes." Addi inhaled. "She was inconsolable. She declined any offer to stay with either Mom and Dad or me. I saw her at the reading of the will. Sky left everything she had to me and just a letter to her."

"Wow, just a letter?" Josh glanced at Addi. "That's something. I wonder why. Sky was her only living child. First Uncle Stan now Sky. She is alone in this world. It's crazy."

Addi leaned back in the chair and closed her eyes. "Yes. Crazy. It's always a drain on the ones left behind."

"Yup." Josh cleared his throat. "You didn't tell me about your regrets."

Addi opened her eyes and looked at him. "What?"

"I just told you that I still have feelings for lying, cheating Ellie who cheated on me and wrung me out to dry even though I have a perfectly good wife at home, but you didn't say anything to me about what your regrets are."

Addi swallowed. "Josh..."

"That's my name." Josh grinned. "Come on Dr. Addison Porter, what are your regrets?"

"It's not something I talk about ever." Addi inhaled. "You wouldn't understand."

Josh laughed. "What, you killed someone? You are secretly gay? Nothing can shock me these days, 2017 is the year of the unshockable Josh."

"I have been seeing Randy Vassell for the past twenty

years," Addi said it in a rush. "I return to Jamaica every year to see him. We meet at my apartment in Mobay. Sometimes he comes to New York.

"Five years ago, I had a miscarriage, right about the time when Kenya had Chad. We've been going downhill since then. Last year he broke it off with me. He said he just could not do it anymore."

Josh slowed down significantly. The unshockable Josh was shocked. "You have an apartment in Mobay?"

Tears came to Addi's eyes. She had forgotten that was how Josh reasoned. He processed the lighter data first.

"Yes, I do. Bought it twelve years ago."

"Randy is my best friend." His voice was husky. His hand trembled on the steering wheel. "He loves Kenya. He is faithful to her or so I thought.

"They are the ideal, Addi. Everybody knows that Randy and Kenya are the ideal... Tell me you are joking."

Addi wasn't prepared for the pain that this statement evoked. She had thought herself immune from the little twinges of guilt.

Randy was a popular evangelist, celebrated the world over as a man of God, a stalwart in the morality stakes, an example while the people of his generation were going to hell in a handbasket.

And she was his lover.

Had been his lover. She corrected quickly. They were over. Finally, completely over. Twenty years of being faithful to a married man who wouldn't leave his wife because he was too much of a coward to do so.

"Randy and Kenya were never a love match." She gritted out at her shell-shocked brother. "He married her because everyone was pressuring him to! Including you, I remember. I was there. He loved me. Me!"

"Don't tell me you were seeing him when you were a teenager. When I brought him home for weekends and that summer, he stayed at the house..." Josh frowned at her, "I caused this, didn't I?"

"No, you didn't," Addi said tiredly. "Randy got married to further his career. He thought that he would forget his feelings for me. He didn't. I didn't. We couldn't unlove one another..."

"How...How did this start?" Josh stammered.

"Summer of 92," Addi said tiredly.

"You were fifteen!" Josh bellowed. "He never..."

"No." Addi fanned him off. "No need to sound so outraged. Randy is not a perv'. I am now sorry I told you. I knew you couldn't handle it."

"It's a shocker, that's all. Maybe I am not so unshockable after all. But I don't think there was any indication, even back then about you and Randy. I must have been blind."

"Your hands were full with Ellie. Wasn't that the summer you fell head over heels in lust?" Addi grunted, "Sky was busy with her Rusty crush. Mom was busy with the store and Dad, and Uncle Stan were busy with the new construction. Aunt Ivy was busy with whatever she was busy with. I only had Randy for company all summer when he came to work for Dad at the business.

"Nobody knew. Not even Sky. I never did tell her. She always thought I came back to Jamaica so often because you were here."

Josh exhaled heavily. "The summer of regrets."

Addi shrugged. "I don't regret knowing Randy."

"You wasted twenty years of your life having an illicit affair with him," Josh said heavily. "Why deny it? If you had a do-over, you would change things, wouldn't you?"

"Yes. Maybe…" Addi glanced at him. "I don't know. What

would you change?"

"That's easy." Josh snorted. "Find the guy who got Ellie pregnant and punch him to death."

"Be serious." Addi clutched the urn tighter to her.

"I don't know." Josh shrugged. "It happened already, can't change now, can it? What's the use rehashing the past?"

Chapter Two

They drove in relative silence to Mandeville. Josh turned on the radio to a station that was playing only R and B music. He glanced at her once or twice and shook his head in disappointment.

Addi ignored him. She had spent two decades chastising herself about her lifestyle. And she wasn't going to start today, not when the affair was over. Every year she had made a vow to move on. Promising herself that that year would be it and then Randy would call.

I love you...I miss you. Please come back to me.

He was like an addictive substance. Even now she had to limit the time she gave herself to dwell on him.

She had gone to a therapist to figure out how to give him up, but no therapist, no self-help book, no fervent prayers had cured her of Randy Vassell.

He was the one who ended their twenty- year- long affair, last year, February 2016.

It probably would never have been her. She was weak and pathetic, and she still thought about him.

Even now.

Especially now, when they were on Jamaican soil. In his backyard so to speak. He had moved to Mandeville permanently ten years ago after building her dream home.

The house she had found the plan for, drooled over, shared with him. He had taken it and built it, and now his wife was living in it with him. It was enough to make a girl howl in frustration.

"I want to see it," she said out loud when Josh turned at the stoplights to head to the town area.

"You want to see what?" Josh frowned at her.

"I want to see Randy's house in real life. I have always seen it in pictures. I haven't been back to this side of Jamaica since I left twenty-one years ago."

"That's not a good idea," Josh muttered. "It's in a gated community. I can't just enter the place without permission."

"So get permission," Addi growled. "I am never coming back to this place after today. It won't matter."

Josh glared at her. "You are obsessed. He is probably not at home anyway."

"I just want to see my dream house that's all."

"Your dream house?" Josh snorted. "I should have known. While he was building Kenya constantly complained that she had no say in any of the design."

"That's because it was mine. It was supposed to be our house. Kenya is living my life."

"No." Josh gritted out. "Kenya is living her life. You were supposed to be living yours! I can't tell you how disappointed I am in you right now, Addi. I thought I knew you, but I am beginning to believe that I don't know anything anymore. Sky, you, everybody, my gosh!"

"You still love your ex-wife, and I am pretty sure your current wife doesn't know how you feel." Addi snapped. "You have no right to talk to me about how I feel."

"Touché," Josh muttered. "Let me drive up there. On the off chance that he is home, you'll see your dream house."

Addi turned to look through the window. She pulled her sweater closer. It had gotten progressively chillier the closer they drove to Hope Vale, the place where Randy had his house.

It wasn't very far from where they used to live either. The Hope area had changed beyond recognition.

Where there was pastureland was now built up communities. Each house looked like it was competing with the others in size and design.

Mandeville was known for its cool climate compared to the rest of Jamaica, and for its returning resident population. She could see evidence of this in the new communities they were passing through.

Josh stopped at a tall, black, iron gate that had intricate designs bent and artfully arranged on it. A sign at the bottom of the gate read: 'Automatic gate stand clear'. There was a small security outpost with two guards.

Josh rolled down his window, the security standing near their side of the gate walked up to the car.

"I am here to see Randall Vassell. My name is Josh Porter."

The security guard nodded, went back inside her station and made a call. A few seconds later the gate started opening.

"I guess he is here then," Josh muttered. "I could use a bathroom break."

Addi swallowed. He was here. She hadn't seen him in a year, and he was here. "We don't have to get out of the car," she said, her voice had a tremor to it. She hoped Josh didn't pick up on it. "I just want to see the house."

"You can stay in the car. I need to use the bathroom," Josh said. "It is becoming somewhat urgent."

Addi rolled her eyes. "Okay. You visit them often?"

"Yes," Josh said grudgingly as if he was finding conversation with her difficult. "They have a lovely clubhouse down that way." He pointed down a palm-lined street. "We kept Nancy's eighth birthday party here last month."

"She liked the gift I sent?" Addi's voice was husky. She cleared her throat.

"When we get to the house this evening, you can ask her, but from what I could see she did." He turned into a cobbled stone driveway of a beige colored house with brown trimmings. The walls were low; some yellow and pink flowers were planted at the border of a large lawn.

"Here is your dream house," Josh said softly. "Got to give it to you, it is a nice design. You have taste. I need to use the bathroom."

Josh got out and no sooner had he pressed the buzzer the door was flung opened, and there he was, Randall Vassell, the third—all six-foot one inch of him, looking the same as he did last year when he had told her that he couldn't live a lie anymore.

Josh must have said something to him; he looked straight at her in the car. It wasn't long before he was heading towards her, his long strides eating up the driveway. His confidence was palpable. He was a big guy, muscular, hulking. He had bulked up since the last time she saw him.

He had probably amped up his workouts because his biceps were bulging underneath the red shirt that was stretched across his wide chest. He was clean-shaven, except for a low circle beard. He had dark mahogany skin, straight nose, and chiseled lips. He looked like he usually did—handsome, commanding, and full of presence.

There was a flutter in her heart region that developed into full-fledged palpitations when he came closer and his molasses dark eyes locked with hers through the car window.

Twenty-five years and she still wasn't cured.

He knocked on the glass briefly.

And she wound down the window. Her fingers trembling.

She tucked them into each other. And drummed up a smile. "Hey."

"Hey," his voice was low and husky. "Want to come inside?"

"No." Addi swallowed. "I just wanted to see the house."

"I figured." He shrugged one shoulder. "Kenya is not here. She is gone to a conference in Kingston for three days. You can come and look around."

"I shouldn't." Addi paused.

"I built it all to your specifications," he said roughly, "I painted it exactly how you said..."

"But I don't live in it," Addi said sadly. "How are your children, Togo and Chad?"

"They are fine," Randy said roughly. "Addi, don't do this. Your brother is inside. You are probably feeling overly emotional... I heard about Sky."

Addi swallowed and looked down at the urn.

"That her?" Randy asked gruffly.

"Yep." Addi nodded.

"I can't imagine how you feel." He touched her hand briefly and then pulled it away. "I know how close you two were."

"I am supposed to pour her ashes on the blue stone at the back of the place we used to live." Addi swallowed, "and then read a letter dated for today after I do it. She left me a package with her will. It's all so elaborate."

"And so very Sky-like." Randy smiled sadly. "You were the serious one, and Sky was the drama queen."

"Drama queen to the end," Addi said huskily. "She put on her favorite dress, put on a full face of makeup, then took a whole bottle of sleeping pills."

They stared out together at her dream house silently, neither of them having anything more to say. Addi cleared her throat and leaned back in the car seat.

"I still love you, Addi." He said it softly.

She pretended that she didn't hear. She had spent one whole year weaning herself from thoughts of him. This talk was sure to make her have a relapse.

"You ended it for a reason." She said it as stridently as she could muster. This was for her as well as him. "Chad was in the hospital for asthma, Kenya had a tantrum about you not being there for your family. Your church was being taken over by some rogue pastor, and you were sick and tired of hiding around."

"Yes." He nodded. "Yes. But I am so unhappy without you. I should have left a long time ago."

"You shouldn't have married her in the first place," Addi hissed. "You should have waited for me. You could have. You never wanted to go into ministry anyway. Yet you did. You chose money. You chose power. You chose Kenya over me."

She swiped away the tears flowing down her cheek. "I am over you, Randall Vassell. Over. You. I wish I never met you. I wish I never lost my baby at least I wouldn't be so alone and pathetic."

Randy closed his eyes and swallowed. "Addi, please..."

She turned her head away from him. Breathing ragged gulps of air. Not bothering to stem her sobs when Josh got into the car.

He drove away without a word. It was quite a few minutes before he stopped again and Addi realized that they were parked in the middle of the driveway of the two dwellings.

To the right was her childhood home; it looked freshly painted in white. Somebody had kept up with the garden too. There were some neatly trimmed bougainvilleas in a neat box shape. All of them blooming.

To the left was Uncle Stan's house. It was also well kept and painted in burnt orange. Low purple flowers flanked the driveway giving it a nice contrast.

The brothers, Nathan and Stanley had built identical houses beside each other on the same property separated by a shared driveway. At the back of the dwellings was a small office with a sign that said, Porter Brother's Construction.

Josh looked at her grimly. "There were tenants over at Uncle Stan's until recently. Our place has been empty for a while. Dad did some repairs the other day, said he was planning to sell it."

"He told me." Addi hiccupped.

"I am not going to ask why you were crying," Josh said gruffly. "But know this, I can't be friends with Randy anymore."

"Oh, Josh." Addi got out of the car and stretched. "Don't destroy years of friendship on my account."

Josh snorted. "I can and I will."

Addi grabbed the urn. "It's your call. You will have to tell Kenya and Avery why you guys are on the outs. They are friends, aren't they? You will be breaking up two families, which would be the heights of irony because Randy and I are no longer together."

She took a deep breath.

"Okay, let's get this party started—fulfill Sky's dying wish and head back to my corner of the world where none of this matters."

She walked to the end of the driveway to the edge of the

property where a slab of rock jutted out from the hill.

It was large enough to have an overhang. It was almost cave-like in appearance. Several persons could probably hold under the overhang with ease. At one end of the rocky overhang, the stone had distinct shimmery blue streaks running through it.

They used to fantasize that the streaks were precious jewels trapped in the rock. Uncle Stan had even had a geologist come and assess it. The geologist had declared it ordinary limestone rock, which may have some semi-precious potential.

They had lost interest after the geologist's lackluster declaration. When they were girls, this had been their spot though.

There was a palm-sized engraving etched at the left of the blue rock. In the middle of it, the blue was strongest as if somebody had splashed some paint on it. They had always fantasized that it was somebody's hand forever immortalized in stone.

It was Sky's favorite part of the rock.

Sky would put her hand in the palm and stand there waiting, fantasizing.

Addi searched for it and found the etching of the palm. It was where it always was, partially hidden under a thin bush that had fallen over the side of the bank. She pulled a branch to reveal it fully.

She took a step back and inhaled. "Well Sky, here goes," she muttered.

She unscrewed the top of the urn and started pouring the ashes. Josh watched her from a distance, his mouth set in grim lines.

When Addi finished, she felt as if she should say something, but no flowery speeches came to mind just the cold loneliness that had dogged her since Sky's death.

"Goodbye Sky."

She turned away and headed to the car. She reached for the package that Sky had said in her will, should only be read after scattering her ashes. It was a package within a package within a package.

Josh stood behind her and watched as she pulled away the folds of paper.

"It's a book," she declared when she finally finished pulling the last paper off an ordinary hardcover book, which was taped up at the sides. Obviously, it wasn't for her. There was a bold scrawl in Sky's handwriting, which said, To Be Read by Sky Porter Only.

This was more than odd. Why would Sky address a book to herself? And then leave it to her. It didn't make sense. A letter fell out of the back of the package when she was folding back the papers.

Addi picked up the letter, which had her name, printed on the front of the envelope.

She opened the envelope and started reading.

My darling Cousin Addi,

I know you think I am being extremely inconvenient with all of this high drama. Sprinkling my ashes on blue stones and reading letters after you do it. But there is a reason. You are the only person in the entire world, who I trust to do this. You are the only person who would even countenance what I am about to say. So listen to me carefully. Don't dismiss me Addi! This is important.

Remember Monica Campbell, the quiet lady who lived beside us on the hill. One day she told me something, I never told a soul. I thought she was crazy, to be honest. She told me that her grandmother could time travel if she wanted. She said that there were four-time portals in Jamaica. All of them connected to stones. The blue stone on our land is one of the portals. You can only travel once in your lifetime.

And, only special people can travel. Only the people with a distinct T in the lines of their palms can do it. You have that T, Addi. Most people have five main lines in their hands you have two. Just two. It is obvious that you are different. It is obvious that you are one of them.

Every Sunday when we meet for brunch, I have wanted to tell you about this, but I know that you would laugh it off. We are not people who believe in all of this madness, but every time I see the T in your palms, I wonder.

And that is why I requested that you bring my ashes here to be scattered. I knew you would do it.

There are things that I have been hiding. Oh Addi, forgive me. I suffered through a special kind of hell these last couple of weeks. I couldn't taint you with it. I couldn't tell a soul. Even my expensive therapist. It all began in the summer of 92. I need you to go back there. I need you to stop it before it began. I need you to fix things for me. I need you to fix me. I am broken. I am broken beyond repair and this year, 2017, I decided that I couldn't go on. I need your help. I have a notebook attached to this package, when you go back you need to give it to the young Sky. You need to insist that she read it. You need to make her believe it.

Monica told me that all you need to do to travel in your own lifetime is to place your palm on the blue stone, imagine the year you want to go to, and you'll get there. This is our do-over Addi. It is worth a shot. Save me. Save our family. Please.

Your cousin and friend,
Sky

Chapter Three

Addi folded the letter and looked into her palm. She didn't pay attention to her palms. Why would she? She had two clear lines in her hands and no intersecting lines. It had never been an issue before this mad letter.

"Let me see your palms!" she called to Josh who was peering into the house, his hand cupped around the glass windows to get a better view inside.

"What?" Josh looked up at her.

"Your palms," Addi said impatiently. "Let me see them."

Josh held up his hands and walked over to her. "What's this about?"

Addi held up her hands, and he looked at them and raised an eyebrow. "What?"

"I only have two lines in my palms. Yours look more like an M, mine looks like a T."

"Ah," Josh nodded. "So you are an alien? I always suspected it."

"No silly, "Addi wriggled her fingers at him. "Sky thinks that there is a special reason why I have only two lines in my palms. I can time travel."

"Sure." Josh mused. "Why not?"

"No laughter. No snicker. No protests." Addi touched his forehead. "You okay?" Feeling feverish?"

"I am quite fine." Josh leaned on the car. "However, I think that Sky was not okay, that's why she killed herself. And you, I think that you are grieving. Because there is no way that you are taking any of this seriously.

"You are the woman who has a Ph.D. Obviously, your love life was a mess, so I am not sure about your judgment, especially where men are concerned, but I kind of expect better from you, Addi. You know, it is expected since you are the bright one and all."

Addi sighed and leaned beside him on the car. "Yay me, bright Addi with the Ph.D."

She folded her arms and looked out at the landscape.

Not much had changed on their street. In front of their house was an open lot with quite a few pink fleshed guavas growing wild over there. They used to raid the trees when they were children. Her mom would make jam and jellies and juices.

To the left of them were the Jones'. The poor Jones'. Every year it had seemed as if Mrs. Jones had a new baby.

Her father and uncle had tried to use Mr. Jones in their business so that he could have a steady income, but the man was no good at the jobs assigned to him. Her parents had settled for having him occasionally garden instead.

She wondered where they were now. The two-story bungalow house where they used to live seemed empty.

The house was the same non-descript green color that always looked as if it could do with a lick of paint. The yard looked unkempt, and the larger than average garage where Mr. Jones used to tinker with his old car was filled with junk.

"Where are they now?" Addi asked pointing at the Jones' place.

"Don't know." Josh shrugged. "I heard that the oldest girl, I think her name was Joy, became a lawyer. And one of the boys was something in athletics a couple years ago."

Addi smiled. "Good for them. Why did we never get to know the Jones'? Especially the wife, she had seemed nice."

"You can't be friends with everybody."

"But they were our neighbors." Addi pinched Josh. "We should have made an effort. Even though it was a small community, we had lived insular lives, didn't we?"

Josh smirked. "Add that to your list of regrets—the living of an insular life."

Addi nodded. "Maybe I will."

She looked to the right of them. On a hill was a sprawling white Victorian style house that had a large wrap around veranda to take advantage of the view. There was a long winding driveway that led up to the house.

The cut stonewalls bordering the driveway was flanked by the breathtaking shrub called Yesterday, Today and Tomorrow. The purple and white flowers were prolific and distinct against the stonework, and the shrubs seemed to extend all the way to the top of the impressive entrance of the house.

It was where Monica Campbell lived. She was the one who told Sky tales of time travel. Addi turned around and looked up at the house fully. It looked the same. Well-kept. Imposing. And then she saw movement on the veranda, like a person going in and out of the front door.

She straightened up from the car.

"Does Monica Campbell still live over there?" she asked

her brother who had gone silent. He was staring in front of him with a frown as if he was considering unpleasant things.

"Yes." Josh roused himself from his painful contemplations and focused on her. "Why?"

"I want to go and see her. It won't hurt."

"Want me to drive?" He looked at her green wedge shoes. They had seemed to be a good idea when she was leaving her apartment to head to the airport.

She had only packed for two days. The intention had been to come to Jamaica, spread the ashes and then get out of the country as fast as she could.

Now here she was actually contemplating Sky's letter. At least she would have a conversation with Monica confirm that her cousin had been losing it and then head back to Kingston with Josh.

"Want me to drive up to the Campbell's residence?" Josh asked repeating himself, longsuffering resignation in his voice.

"Yes." She nodded. "Yes."

"I won't ask why." Josh opened her side of the car door. "I am done asking questions just consider me a casual observer in your clown show."

Addi suppressed a sigh and got into the vehicle. "Thank you," she said when he started the car.

****

Monica Campbell was in her early sixties but didn't look it. She had gotten plumper from what Addi remembered of her. She still had that elegant way to move her body as if she were an unhurried lady of the manor.

She was tall and dark with long relaxed hair dyed in a purple tint, it rippled around her shoulders whenever she moved her head.

She was sitting on the veranda when they drove up, a box of plant cuttings at her feet.

She greeted them warmly enough, offered them a seat on one of her padded chairs and sat across from the two of them, a grin on her face.

"You two look the same!" She announced looking between Addi and Josh with her eyes sparkling. "I would recognize you both anywhere and I haven't seen you since you were children."

Addi smiled. "Well, teenagers...the family left Jamaica when I was eighteen."

"Yes. I remember." Monica nodded. "Your father waited until you finished high school. Josh was already married."

She smiled at Josh and asked innocently. "Where is your wife, what was her name again?"

"Ellie," Josh said abruptly. "We are divorced."

"Oh." Monica looked sorrowful. "I am so sorry to hear."

"It was ages ago." Josh shrugged like it didn't matter but he was holding himself stiffly in the chair like he was ready to bolt any minute now.

"So, what can I help you with, Miss Addison?" Monica turned to Addi.

Addi inhaled and then stuttered, "This is going to sound strange. Well this is... er... a..."

Monica raised her eyebrows at every hesitation.

"Sky, remember Sky?"

"Oh yes." Monica nodded, "Of course I remember Sky. Last year when she came to Jamaica, we had a long chat."

"You saw her last year?" Addi squeaked.

"Yes," Monica said thoughtfully, "she had a lot of questions about..."

Monica pursed her lips. "Sky was here for the release of

that young man, Rusty from prison. She came here quite distressed after speaking to him. How is she now?"

"She... er," Addi cleared her throat. "She is dead."

"Oh," Monica froze, a shocked frozen look on her face. "That's...I don't know what to say... "

"She said you knew about time travel and the blue stone in our yard." Addi stopped speaking…she sounded ridiculous.

Josh was looking at her and shaking his head like he couldn't believe that she had brought it up with Monica, a perfectly sane-looking woman.

"Ah," Monica nodded. "I wonder if...."

She shook her head as if to dispel that thought, "Yes. I told Sky the legend of the pathways. She asked me about it."

"The legend of the pathways?" Josh repeated, the cynicism was rolling off his tongue.

"Oh yes," Monica was unperturbed by his attitude. "Since the beginning of time, there have been special babies born with a mark in their palms.

"A simple cross, a 'T' if you will. These human beings are capable of going back in time, never forward.

"Always back and only once. They can reset the timeline, change what they want to change if they can, but they can only travel in their lifetime and only if they can find the pathways to connect to. My grandmother referred to these people as the resetters.

"When a resetter finds a pathway all they need to do is picture the time they want to go back to, place their palms on the pathway and sure enough they will be there, in their younger bodies. For a time, they will retain memories from the timeline they are traveling, but the longer they stay in the new timeline, the more memories of the old one will fade until they can barely remember the things that went on before. It will be a faint, fuzzy dream. Resetters have to move fast if they are going to accomplish anything. I guess it's kind of like having a vague feeling that you've lived a life before or been someplace before."

Josh made a coughing sound.

Monica continued. "The pathways are usually made of stone. I don't know why. Maybe because some of the stones we so casually pass by have been around since the beginning of time."

Josh coughed again and looked at Addi.

Addi tried to ignore him.

Monica smiled. "I see Josh is not a believer."

"Neither am I to be honest," Addi said gently. "Monica, I liked your story. It sounds very... er..."

"Sensational." Monica chuckled. "I understand. I wasn't a believer either when my grandmother used to tell us her stories."

"But you are a believer now?" Addi asked cautiously.

"Yes," Monica smiled. "I gradually accepted that it is possible. My grandma had a diary in which she recorded research she had done on resetters throughout the years."

Josh got up and stretched. "I am going to sit in the car. It was lovely to see you again, Monica."

Monica smiled. "And you too Josh."

Addi and Monica watched as he walked away.

"Sorry about his rudeness." Addi sighed. "Today was a bit overwhelming for us. I scattered Sky's ashes by the blue stone as she requested."

"I can imagine so." Monica clutched her hand. "Can you do me a favor, Addi?"

"What?" Addi looked at where their hands were joined.

"When you go back, come and find me. Sky said she was asking you to go to the summer of 92?"

"Yes." Addi didn't know why but she felt a shiver of fear.

"Were you the one who put her up to this, Monica? Were you the reason she...?"

"No!" Monica looked at Addi in horror. "She believed the stories I told her. She was the one who asked me about time travel. She seemed very distressed at the time. My stories did seem to calm her down.

"But I had no idea what she would do...I didn't tell her to go and kill herself and force you to reset things. I wouldn't do that!"

Addi nodded. She believed Monica. Her eyes begged her to believe.

Addi exhaled. At any rate she knew Sky. Nobody could convince Sky to do anything that she didn't want to do.

"I'll give you my grammy's diary to read when you go back to 92." Monica inhaled shakily. "A couple years ago my brother cleared out her old room and threw away everything. Remind me when you go back not to let him clear out her room."

Addi shook her head, "Monica..."

"And remind me of this," Monica said her expression intent, "on August 5, 1995. I will marry Walter Sparks. Warn me not to do it. He is not straight and had no business asking me to marry him. He is a lonely man trying to do the right thing and I got caught up in his mess. Warn me, Addi. I wasted a good five years of my life."

"Monica, this is crazy!" Addi whispered fiercely. "This is a fairytale fantasy, time traveling...resetting is madness!"

Monica held Addi's hand and looked at the two lines in her palms. "You are a resetter. It's obvious. You can only go back once. Make it count, Addison Porter. Remember the date, I asked you about. And warn me about Walter. I would like at least one child. I always regretted not having any children. Prompt me to get moving on that, okay."

Addi pulled away her hand and walked toward the car. "Goodbye, Monica."

Monica nodded. "There is no harm in trying this fairytale fantasy, Addi. Put your palm on that blue stone, picture the summer of 92 and relive your life."

Addi went into the car.

"I am starving," Josh said. "Want us to stop at a fast food place before we head into town?"

"Yes. Sure." Addi nodded. "I want to give the place a last look over though."

She got out of the car when Josh drove up to it. "This won't take a minute."

She reassured him, his long-suffering expression was cracking, and he was practically scowling at her.

"I'll soon be back." She grabbed the book with her that was addressed to Sky. If for some reason this resetting business worked, and she could time travel she wanted to take the book with her.

She tucked it firmly under her arm.

Josh growled. "Don't be long."

Addi walked to the rocky overhang, she fitted her right palm into the blue rock and with her other hand she pressed the book on and her other palm on the rock.

She closed her eyes and pictured the beginning of summer 1992. It was the day after her final exam and she was lying in her bed staring up at the ceiling and wondering what she would do with that summer. She remembered that day so vividly.

The rock started feeling warmer, there was a tingling in her fingers, she almost drew them away in shock but the world around her was losing focus and she felt a floating sensation.

Chapter Four

"**A**ddi, you okay?" Josh sounded concerned.

She was still at the blue stone with her hand in the groove, clutching Sky's book.

"She is taking up my bad habits." Sky said before she could turn around. "I like that spot."

Addi slowly spun around. The book fell from her hand with a thud.

"I wanted you to meet my friend from university," Josh said pushing his hand in his pocket. A young Josh, tall, thin, clean-shaven, no lines in his face. No paunch around the waistline. No droop to his mouth. Handsome.

And Sky, she was standing beside him in a jeans shorts and a blue t-shirt with fringes all around it. The words Miami Vice splashed across the front.

Her brown hair was in two fat plaits crisscrossed in a crown style on her head. Sky had hated that her hair was that color. Addi had forgotten entirely about it looking that way because Sky had started dying it as soon as she could.

Good heavens. What was this? A dream of some sort?

Sky's pretty round face was scrunched up in curiosity as she looked at Addi. It was uncanny the details she could observe in this dream. Her cousin's honey brown skin was flawless except for the gathering of freckles on the bridge of her nose. She was gloriously alive and glaring at Addi because she was not responding.

"What's that?" Sky pointed at the book at her feet.

Addi swallowed.

Her feet.

They were encased in some ugly plastic jelly pink slippers with a bow on the top. She was wearing acid wash shorts and a neon green shirt. Can't Touch This, MC Hammer blazoned across the front.

And she was skinny! And flat chested!

She closed her eyes again and inhaled, any minute now she would awaken from whatever dream this was.

She opened her eyes again and then looked from Sky to Josh. "What year is this?" Her voice, it was different, squeaky, childish.

Sky sniggered and then turned around. "Unlike you, I have my last exam tomorrow. I am going to study. If by any remote chance somebody wants to rescue me from boredom I am in my room. By the way, Josh, your friend is cute. Really cute. You should see him Addi."

She made a swooning motion and then headed to the back door of the other house and closed it.

Josh was left looking at her strangely. "You remember Randall? I told you guys about him."

"Yes." Addi inhaled raggedly. She walked toward Josh and then stopped, looking down at herself.

This was the outfit she had met Randall in the first time.

Back then the date was June the twenty-second, nineteen ninety-two. Maybe it was that date again.

She had time traveled!

She looked in her palm surreptitiously and gasped. She no longer had two lines; she had five and some other lines crisscrossing her palms.

They looked like regular palms!

"What's wrong with your hand, Addi?" Josh was getting impatient with her. Undoubtedly, because she was acting weird.

"Nothing." Addi looked over at him. "I am going to use the bathroom."

"You are leaving your book," Josh said pointing at the book. "When you are done come out and meet Randall. He is going to be doing some accounting for Dad this summer, so he'll be staying with us for three months. He's in the office."

"Sure. Yes." Addi turned back to get the book and then hurried past Josh and into the house. Everything looked familiar and strange at the same time. She almost stumbled as a sense of nostalgia hit her as she walked into the living room. It had red velvet settees, a breakfront with her mother's fake flowers, and gold angel figurines.

She had forgotten how much she hated dusting off the little angel pieces every Friday. A chunky television sat in the middle of the breakfront, no remote in sight. A white telephone sat beside it with the letters JTC printed on top in large fonts. JTC...Jamaica Telephone Company.

Addi couldn't resist picking up the receiver and hearing the dial tone. It was like looking at a relic. She used to make prank calls with this phone.

She put down the phone in the cradle and looked around at the walls. Her mother had a fetish for Air Jamaica Calendars. She still did. She kept it up until the airline was sold. Addi rubbed her temples.

There were some of them now, framed and hanging on the walls. Free gorgeous art. She hadn't appreciated them before. She did so now. She wished that she had collected the Air Jamaica calendars from the nineties.

But wait, she was in the nineties. She was in the nineties! This was no dream. She had really time traveled!

She heard a sound in the kitchen area and she swung around.

The kitchen was at the end of the living room, before that was an alcove with the dining room table, beyond that was the kitchen, a door from the kitchen led to the back and to the office.

"I thought you said you were resting today." Her mother appeared at the kitchen doorway.

"I was. I am," Addi stammered. Her mother looked young! With jet-black hair! It was relaxed and cut in a thick bell cut that swung when she walked.

Her mother had been a seriously attractive woman. Not that she wasn't in the future but in the past Addi had not appreciated how good-looking she was.

This convoluted time traveling business was going to take some to be sorted in her brain.

Addi took her mother in fully. As usual she was dressed immaculately, this time in a charcoal gray suit. She was the manager of the family hardware store that was started by her parents and left in her capable hands when they migrated ten years prior.

That hardware store had gone up in flames in 95, a year before they left Jamaica to be with the grandparents in the States. It was one of the reasons why they left.

Addi moved toward the left of the house. On that side of the house was her and Josh's old bedrooms. They had shared a bathroom.

On the other side were her parents' room and a guest bedroom.

"Oh, Addi." Her mother stopped mid-stride and looked around at her. "A reminder, Randall Vassell is here for the summer. He'll be staying in the guest room. He arrived a while ago. Where were you?"

"By the stone." Addi swallowed. She didn't want to meet Randall for the first time dressed like a clown down on her luck.

" At lunchtime, I'll take something for you two to eat. What do you want?"

Addi shrugged. "Chicken something."

"Okay." Her mother nodded. "Be good. We will have to discuss what you are going to do for your summer."

She headed toward her bedroom and Addi walked towards hers. The door had on a picture of the Hip Hop duo, Kriss Kross.

Addi grimaced. She had been a typical teenager. And that song, Jump was still in heavy rotation in this time.

She opened the door and was greeted by chaos. Books, papers, clothes and posters were strewn everywhere. She had been a slob.

She groaned as she looked at the mess. This was one thing that she had outgrown. Her apartment in Manhattan was tidy, thanks in part to her cleaning service, but she had developed a latent neat streak in college after sharing room with a horrendously untidy girl, who had literally forced her into acting like her mother.

She headed to the closet and paused at the mirror before opening the door. She examined herself closely. She looked absurdly young.

She turned the closet glass toward her as she sat on the

bed. It was a spring bed. It made a squeaking sound when she sat on it. She made a face at herself and then laughed at her reflection in the mirror.

She looked good.

Pure unlined medium brown skin that had never gone through the acne stage. Her cheeks looked a little plumper than they would look in a couple of years, her eyebrows as usual were too thick for her liking—and her hair.

Good Lord! She had forgotten about her hair. It was long, and it was huge. She unraveled it from the single ponytail it was in and laughed. She had forgotten her Rudy Huxtable hair. It was almost to her waist.

By the time she had hit thirty it was barely longer than a finger joint. She had dyed, processed, and abused it to literally within an inch of its life. Now, here it was in all its long and thick, natural unfettered glory.

This time around, she was keeping this lusciousness. She had years of watching YouTube videos and visiting hair sites drooling over the length of other people's natural hair. She would do twist outs and braid outs and wash and go's. The hairstyle experiments were already under her belt. She was not going to try anything new this time around.

She could vaguely remember a fascination with having a bang. That was six months in the future. It had been an unmitigated disaster.

If she was reliving her life, forty was not going to find her hair the same as it was before.

Oh no. This do-over, she was going to be different. Her hair was just the beginning.

She stood in the mirror and turned from side to side. She had a completely flat belly and if her memory served her right, she had eaten any and everything her mind told her to eat.

Oh, to be young again. She felt a niggle of delight. She was enjoying this.

She rifled through her closet and in her chest of drawers. She had very few pieces of sober-looking clothes. She was a fan of bright neon colors at this age. She made a face at the blouses in the drawer.

She vaguely remembered being a fan of the Fresh Prince of Belair and their clothing styles. The show was probably a year old now.

She found a jeans skirt and a white snug fitting top, and she plaited her hair in two and slicked some of her gel at the edges to make it look wavier and then she headed to the back of the house to meet Randall for the first time—again.

"Here she is, my baby sister," Josh said when she pushed the office door open and eagerly walked into the office. She barely registered the interior of the place she wanted to see Randy again, to exult in the fact that after twenty-five years she would be immune. She was not going to be young and naive where he was concerned again. She had seen this man in all his stages.

They had succumbed to their attraction when he had visited New York her second year at college. His first year of marriage to Kenya. He had stayed in her tiny off-campus apartment for two whole weeks making love to her like there was no tomorrow. He hadn't gone to the conference he had been there to attend. He hadn't even pretended that he wanted to go.

And now, with so many years below her belt and so many teachable moments in her life, their eyes connected.

Randy—a younger Randy.

He was twenty! And looked it. Still crazily handsome with his dark eyes and his blinding white smile.

He was smiling at her now. Dimples in his cheek, hand

extended. No recognition in his eyes of her or anything that they had shared together.

Addi backed away. Hell no, she wasn't going through another soul-crushing wringer session with this guy, where just one touch and one look had her forgetting all her principles. No! Not at all.

"Addi!" Josh looked at her in horror as she headed toward the door. "What's wrong with you?"

"Nothing." Addi panted, her heart was racing like she was hurtling toward the ground on a roller coaster ride. "Not one thing."

She opened the door and leaned on the wall outside of it. Everybody knew lightning did not strike twice in the same location.

But that wasn't true was it? Lightning could strike any place more than once. And her helter-skelter rollicking heart rate was proof of that. An attraction to Randy Vassell was obviously not out of the question.

It seemed as if she was wired to like him.

She would spend the rest of the summer out of his way.

She didn't care how rude she looked. This time around she was going to take better care of protecting herself from him. She wanted the dream. And Randy Vassell as magnetic as he was to her wasn't it.

Chapter Five

Addi spent the rest of the day cleaning up her room. Her mother stopped by with food and gave her an appreciative smile.

"Who are you and what have you done with my daughter?" She asked when she came to the door and saw Addi deep into the closet with several odds and ends clustered in neat little piles behind her.

She looked at her mother's smiling face again marveling at how young she was. Her mom would be her age now. Well, her age before she put her hand on that rock and thought about the year 92.

She shook her head from her thoughts, accepted the lunch, gave her mom an impromptu hug and pulled the Kriss Kross poster from the door.

Her mother raised an eyebrow. "Wow."

"Can I get paint to redo my room?" Addi looked at the brash peach paint that was on the wall. "I am thinking yellow.

Like duck yellow."

"Sure." Her mother looked more than pleased. "Are you sure you want to do this by yourself?"

"Yes I am." Addi nodded. "My summer project is to redo my room. Maybe Sky will help."

"Okay. I will take home samples later."

After her mother left, Addi sat in the middle of the floor. She had decided on the spring-cleaning because for one she couldn't remember what she owned in 1992.

Two, she needed to take her mind off her reaction to Randy.

And three, she needed to plan how she was going to go about this resetting business. She didn't want to mess up the future that she knew. She had watched enough time travel stories to know that you had to be careful about what you did now, or things could go horribly wrong.

She wanted to make changes, but she did not want to create rippling changes that would shake the very foundations of society.

She had to give Sky her book and explain to her that it was from the future Sky. She figured that that would be an uphill battle. Sky could sit and listen to a story for a while but after that she would probably laugh her out of the room.

And she didn't want to live the whole teenage experience again. And school! High school. Ugh!

Maybe she could try to learn another language. She had always liked the idea of learning several languages or music. She had a passing fascination with playing the piano at one point in her life.

She glanced at the radio, which was sitting on top of the bookcase overflowing with Nancy Drew, Hardy Boys, and Bobsy Twins books. Under that was a pile of photo romance books that she had craftily hidden below several folders.

She got up and pulled them out. Photo romances were the

heights of the forbidden in her house, but she had acquired a vast collection of them. Most of them were from Sky who had gotten them from Aunt Ivy's hidden trove. She also had a stack of True Confessions in her closet.

Addi dragged them out and sat leaning on the bed while she perused the titles of the stories. My Father Sold Me, Marked For Scandal, I Fell In Love With My Kidnapper.

She would run through those again and the huge collection of old romances her mother had in the bookcase in the music room.

Well, not music room, it had a piano, which was buried under boxes and books and piles and piles of newspaper and old yearbooks, and even construction paraphernalia that could probably be sold at the hardware store.

She remembered helping to clean out that room in 95 when they were leaving for America and how they had marveled at the several things they could have sold.

She would clean it up this summer, maybe have a garage sale, and donate some of the books to the retirement home down the road that had some old ladies that loved to read.

Her previous summer of 92 had not been half as productive. She had spent the summer hanging around Randall, chatting him up in the day. Beseeching him to take her with him on the road. Having dreams and fantasies about him at night. In mid-July, she had grudgingly gone to church camp for two weeks with Sky.

Sky had gotten the flu and then chicken pox in August and had been practically bedridden after camp. She hadn't seen her cousin for the first part of August because she was contagious. Then there had been the murder of Uncle Stan in mid-August on a construction site in Ingleside where both her father and uncle were working. Apparently Rusty had pushed her uncle from the second floor of the building.

She searched in her pile of folder leaves to write down all the possible things that she needed to reset this summer.

Uncle Stan's death. She scribbled that down, grimacing as she saw the chewed-up pen top. She had been gross.

Two, stop Josh from having anything to do with Ellie.

Three, tell Monica Campbell that she should not marry Walter Sparks.

Four, ask Monica for her grandmother's book and find out why my palm is normal again.

Five, give Sky her book and tell her about her future. She put an asterisk beside that one and then wrote— break it to her gently.

Six, avoid Randy. Find somebody else of interest to love. Now, this one was going to be hard.

Seven, find out more about people like me.

She got up and turned on the radio. In 1992 there were only a few radio stations in Jamaica. She turned to Power 106, it was a brand-new station in this year and it played mostly R and B. She sat and stared into space, her mind churning. What could she do with her wealth of knowledge about this era?

How could she make an impact?

She couldn't. She was just a fifteen-year-old girl whose breasts hadn't even exploded into fullness yet. She didn't know any movers or shakers and even if she did no one would listen to her. She was just a girl. She couldn't reset world events. She could only reset her immediate family.

And she should stick to that.

How she would accomplish this noble task. She had no idea. She closed her eyes as Boyz 11 Men, started playing— Although we go, to the end of the road, still I can't let go.

She hummcd to it.

Only opening her eyes when her door was flung opened

unceremoniously. Sky stood in the doorway.

"When I said, I was going to study, I didn't mean all day without a break. You could have come and visited the incarcerated!"

She flung herself across Addi's bed. "Why am I doing Principles of Business? It's not as if I am going to need it later in life. I am going to be a fashion designer."

Addi looked at her, drinking her in. A few days ago, they had found her dead in her apartment, cried over her, chastised themselves over what they could have done differently. She had left a gaping hole in the fabric of her family and yet here she was, young, and vibrant very much alive.

Sky had more than a passing resemblance to Gabrielle Union. She had even given an autograph once pretending to be the actress.

"What are you smiling about?" Sky muttered. Then she raised her head and looked around. "What happened in here?"

"I am sorting out my stuff." Addi grinned. "And then when I am done here, I am going to sort out the music room."

"Boring." Sky muttered covering her eyes. "What do you think of Josh's friend, Randall?"

"He's okay," Addi muttered.

"Are you blind Addison Monique Porter?" Sky squealed the question and then sat up on her elbows and looked at Addi.

"He is the best-looking guy we have ever seen in real life. We should call him chocolate man."

Addi rolled her eyes.

"You like him, and you are just pretending," Sky said putting on a long-suffering tone. She spotted Addi's forgotten lunch resting on the dresser and jackknifed out of bed.

"Why didn't Aunt Vicky take lunch for me?"

Addi shrugged. "You can have it, I am not hungry."

"Cool." Sky started eating and then put the lunch box back on the dresser when, Would I Lie To You by Charles and Eddie came on.

"I have to dance to this," She said her eyes lighting up. "Come on, Addi. This is our jam!"

Addi shook her head. "No!"

"Yes!" Sky swung her hips and sang to the music, "would I lie to you baby? Would I lie to you? Oh yea!"

Addi got up. She had forgotten this song. The 90s had good songs going for it that was for sure.

She danced with Sky. Stomping on her magazines and papers and clothes strewn across the floor. It was good to be fifteen again, at least for the time being.

****

Addi finished sorting out her final pile of teenage debris. She had been a little hoarder. Some of the things she was packing up for the garbage the first time around she had thought she couldn't do without. To her shame she still had a dozen plush toys arranged all around the room. She bagged them and was just about to haul the garbage bag filled with toys when she entered the living room and saw Randall.

He was sitting in the settee looking outside when she noisily entered the living room. She stopped when she saw him and gave him a full scowl.

He had the audacity to smile.

"Addison."

"Randall." Addi smirked.

"Need help?" He asked ignoring her hostility.

"No." Addi almost hissed her response.

Randy nodded. "Okay."

She passed him and headed onto the veranda. Her mother had her boxes of stuff that she frequently gave away to charity in one of the corners. She put her bag on top of two boxes and the bag became untied. One of her teddy bears fell out.

"Giving away your bears?" Randy asked. He had followed her and leaned on the wall watching her lazily.

"None of your business," Addi muttered as she stuffed the offending thing back in the bag.

"What did I do to you?" Randy asked puzzled. "You are so hostile, like a wild untamed cat."

Addi swung around and looked at him fiercely. "In a previous time, you and I were lovers. You broke my heart. My hostility stems from the fact that in this timeline you and I will mean nothing to each other. You are going to leave me alone. I will leave you alone. I will move on with my life the way I am supposed to this time around."

Randy looked shocked. He shook his head a little. "You have quite an imagination going on there don't you, Addison?"

"Yes." Addi tied the bag more aggressively than she needed to and then stomped past him. "Stay away from me!"

Randy nodded firmly as if she had no need to give him any warning. "I will. Definitely."

"Good." She huffed and went back to her room. The place looked more to her liking now—minimal products on the dresser and her closet was better arranged. Most of her garish clothes were packed away in a charity box.

Her study table was now clean of books and papers, her bookcase arranged according to the size of the books and posters removed from her wall. She had long outgrown the nineties. She hoped she could outgrow Randall as well.

Chapter Six

Addi had forgotten that family dinner was a major production in her family. Her mother had cooked steamed cabbage and salted fish with rice. She was expected to set the table with the proper utensils and mix the drinks, which was Kool-Aid. She could choose any flavor she wanted from a large box of packets in the cupboard.

She had quit all sugary drinks years ago. It was with fascination that she looked at the giant Kool-Aid box and contemplated the flavors.

"There is still apple left," her mother reminded her when she saw her dithering over the flavors. "Apple is still your favorite, right?"

"Yes, it was. It is," Addi said quickly pulling out an apple-flavored packet.

She was fishing lemon seeds from the drink when her father walked into the kitchen. He grabbed her mother from behind and kissed her soundly.

Then he pulled Addi's hair. "Hey kid."

"Hi Dad."

Addi smiled. He aged pretty well. Twenty-five years in the future he wore his hair clean-shaven to hide the grays and a bald spot in the middle of his head. He was almost the same size now too—slim and wiry and tall. Not a slouch to his ramrod straight back now or in the future.

Today his hair was big, bushy, and in an Afro. He wore a full beard. Her dad had loved his beard. She searched her mind trying to remember when he had stopped wearing it. When it got too gray. She remembered him complaining about that.

He was a good-looking man, with a slight exotic slant to his eye from an Asian ancestor. He had dark rich mahogany skin and a straight nose that flared at the end from a maroon ancestor and a warm ready smile that was all him.

Josh resembled her dad more closely than she had thought. Looking at him now, the resemblance was glaring.

She got his nose, but the medium brown skin tone and the forehead and the shape of her lips from her mom.

"How was your day?" He asked Addi as he pushed a glass under the tap and filled it with water.

"Good. I cleaned up my room."

"It's amazing our Addi is turning into an exemplary young woman." Her mother smiled. "She is even giving away some of her stuff to charity."

"You are?" Her father smiled his eyes warm and playful.

"And she wants to paint it." Her mother continued. "I brought home some samples for her to choose from."

"It's the construction gene in her bones." Her father nodded. "If you want to come and help out on the site, I can arrange it..."

"No," her mother protested before he could finish. "No girl

of mine is going on any construction site to work. She is a girl!"

Her father shrugged. "Girls can do anything. She can paint her room, it's only logical to expect that she can build a house."

He winked at Addi. "You are not the weaker sex. You are strong. Don't forget that."

"Thanks, Dad." She smiled at her father. He was the same as always.

Her mother made a sound of disgust. "I don't want a tomboy. And I hate that you put insane notions in her head."

"Not insane notions, Vicky. I just want one of our kids to run the construction business when Stan and I can't manage anymore. Josh is already at the hardware store with you, Sky is a girly girl. Now Addi is my only hope."

Her mother chuckled. "Nice try. Go wash up for dinner."

****

Dinner was a lively affair, despite the fact that Randall was sitting across from her at the table and trying to avoid eye contact with her.

Her father recounted a story about one of his workers, and Randy reported that he was just filing receipts and other bills for the day. He was nowhere near starting to do the real accounting. Her mother asked her about some end of school term related program that parents were supposed to attend. Addi couldn't answer. She had no recollection of anything related to the school from 1992.

The conversation turned to Josh after a brief pause. And he, with a big smile and obvious naivety announced to the table. "Today I met the woman who is going to be my wife! I mean, I met her before, but today she finally responded to me."

Vicky laughed and clapped her hands.

Nate looked contemplatively on his son and shook his head. "Really, Josh? One conversation and you are declaring her to be wife."

Randy smiled and patted his friend on the back.

Addi sat up straighter in her chair. Things just got serious; Josh's biggest regret was about to start.

"Yes Dad." Josh chuckled. "I am the age you were when you married Mom. You said you took one look at her and you could feel the forever vibes. Well, it is the same with me. I took one look at Ellie and I know. I think I have always known we would be something. Today she reciprocated."

"One look?" Addi snorted.

"Yes, one look." Josh glared at her. "What's gotten into you today?"

Addi subsided in her chair. Her parents would soon ask what he meant and then she would be in for a cussing. She didn't have long to wait.

"What do you mean Josh?" Vicky looked from her to Josh.

Randy was the one who rescued her. "She thinks I look like some character in a book she is reading and refused to shake my hand earlier today. We cleared that up this evening."

"Oh." Vicky chuckled. "Addi, please don't mix up reality and fiction. I know I encourage you to read but you should always be polite."

"Yes ma'am." She nodded trying to avoid looking at Randy. It was a good save. He probably thought his explanation was true too. Damn him for rescuing her. This did not change a thing.

"So Josh, how on earth did you meet this Ellie girl? You were in the office all day." Vicky turned back to Josh. "Give us all the details."

Josh smiled. "When I went to pick up lunch at Mack J's, remember? She is Mack's niece. She's been working with him for the year, part-time. She is going to culinary school. She says she wants to be a chef."

"You have two years left of university," Nate said gruffly, pointing his fork at Josh. "Finish school before you think of marriage and get to know this girl properly before you even consider getting serious."

Josh nodded but Addi could see he was in the first throes of attraction. She had to do something to fix this and fast or her poor brother would get hurt again.

****

Addi couldn't sleep. She always had an issue with falling asleep in a new place. This part of her life was so long ago she had completely forgotten how it felt. Her bed had springs and it squeaked at every turn, the pillows were overstuffed, and the sheets were rough feeling.

And there were little noises around the house that made sleeping difficult—like the lizard croaking outside her window and the sound of the wind moving through the trees.

There was a willow near the front and she could hear the haunting whoo hoo noise that it made as it played with the wind. She looked at the clock. It was fifteen minutes after twelve and it was chilly.

She had forgotten how cool it was even in the summer. She went in the closet for her sweatshirt and socks and tried to make herself feel comfortable, but it wasn't happening.

She opened her door and looked outside. The lights were off. Only the glare from the side light on Uncle Stan's house reflected in the living room.

The hall clock's ticking sounded loud in the stillness of

the night and she could hear the dripping of the tap in the kitchen. She headed to one of the settees and almost jumped out of her skin when she saw a silhouette sitting in the settee.

"Just me," Randy whispered holding up a glass of water in his hand. "Not a ghost." He was dressed in a tracksuit bottom and a matching long sleeved heather gray top.

"Oh," she walked around the settee and sat across from him. "Can't sleep?"

"Not a wink." Randy chuckled. "New bed. No sleep. What about you?"

"Same." Addi shrugged.

"You are still sticking to your time travel story, huh?" Randy grinned she could see his teeth in the half dark.

"Yep," Addi murmured. "Because it's true and I can make a pretty accurate prediction as to why you can't sleep tonight, and it has nothing to do with being in a new bed."

"Okay, I bite. Why can't I sleep?" Randy put his glass on the center table and leaned toward her. He was humoring her.

Addi decided to shock him.

"You are a scholarship kid. You got a B on your calculus exam last semester and you are not sure if you will be considered for the scholarship next year. They are strict about the grades and decision time is coming up."

Randy was frowning now, his mouth slightly agape. He was holding himself like somebody who was not sure what to say.

"Your grandmother will call here tomorrow to tell you good news, so you can stop worrying."

"There is no way you..." Randy stammered. "How do you know this?"

"I am a time traveler. A resetter. I have lived this summer before. I had this same conversation with you before. Only difference between now and the other time is that, in the other time, we were at dinner. You told us how anxious you were before your grandmother called and how elated you were that you did get the scholarship for the next school year."

Randy rubbed his hand over his face. "Addi, you are so imaginative it's frightening. I know Josh must have made some of this slip. I told him about the grade and the scholarship."

"Did you tell him about the birthmark on your lower back three inches to your left butt cheek?" Addi chuckled, "or the fact that your first time was with a woman named Freda, your grandmother's neighbor. You enjoyed yourself, but you are still not sure it wasn't rape because she was fifty and you were just thirteen...."

Randy snapped his head up to look at her. "How the hell…?"

His question was harsh almost loud in the silence.

"Nobody knows that." His hands were trembling. He actually looked a little afraid of her.

Addi felt remorseful at her shock tactics. She was using private, confidential conversations they had and was laying it bare in the open. She doubted that he had told anyone else this. They had been so close.

She sighed. She needed to get over her anger at Randy. This Randy hadn't hurt her yet. He wouldn't get the chance to this time around. This Randy hadn't even met Kenya. This Randy was barely a man. He was just a second-year university student who was coming from a tragic background, who was trying to get through life like anybody else.

She closed her eyes. "Sorry Randy."

"How do you know these things, Addi? The Freda thing was a secret. I mean, I never told a soul about her. Not my parents nor my grandmother..."

"I know these things because you told me all of it."

"I have never met you until yesterday and you can't be a time traveler," Randy whispered. "That is not possible. Time is linear, there is no jumping around in it."

"Say's who?" Addi challenged him," somebody told you this and you believed them."

"It doesn't make sense," Randy argued. "If it were possible why isn't everybody doing it?"

"Because only resetters can go back in time, resetters are special people with a T in their palms. They can't go forward in time only back in their lifetime," Addi said patiently. She understood where he was coming from with his argument, she was there too just a day ago. "And they can only travel if they encounter specific pathways."

"Resetters... pathways." Randy sighed, "So where are these pathways?"

"There are only a few left in Jamaica or at least that's what I heard," Addi said. "One happens to be on our land. Amazing, isn't it?"

"Yes." Randy nodded. "Very."

He didn't believe a word she was saying. There was silence for a while as he sipped slowly on his water. Addi admired him in the half-light. She couldn't decide who was more appealing, young Randy or older Randy.

He was and always would be a gorgeous man but the younger version of him had an air of innocence that was somewhat appealing. Maybe it was that earnest way he had of talking now. Earnest. Eager. He had lost that, gotten more serious and measured and mature.

"How did you know about my birthmark?"

He asked the question out of the blue.

"We were lovers for a long time. I know about your birthmark and more." Addi yawned. "I could write a book on

Randall Vassell."

"You really are imaginative." Randy got up and stretched.

"That may be true," Addi said sleepily, 'but what I said tonight will haunt you. How could I possibly know the things about you that I do? And tomorrow when your grandmother calls and gives you the news about your scholarship you'll be even more confused."

Randy pushed his hands into his pockets, rocked back on his heels and regarded her for a while. "Goodnight, Addi."

"Night." Addi snuggled closer into the settee cushions. The couch was more comfy than her bed. She closed her eyes, finally succumbing to exhaustion.

****

"I aced the POB exam!" Sky entered her room with a bounce to her steps. "I killed it. I did it in thirty minutes. I might have to reconsider business as a career. The principles of business is easy peasy."

Addi grunted, she hadn't left her room all day. She was eagerly running through her mother's box of old romance novels, trying to avoid Randy. She knew his grandmother had called to tell him about the scholarship, she heard when the phone rang and then the knock on her door. She didn't answer. She was feeling somewhat remorseful. If she should have revealed her time traveling to anyone it should have been Sky. She was the one who practically sent her back here.

She looked up from her book when Sky threw herself across the bed, still in her uniform.

"Now what are we going to do for the summer," Sky said turning on her back and looking up into the ceiling. "What can we possibly do in this boring slow corner of country that we live in?"

"I have no idea," Addi said in awe. "I never thought of how utterly boring this time in my life was."

Sky turned her head to look at her. "You lived another life, Missy?"

"Yes Missy." Addi chuckled. "I did."

She looked at Sky whose face was as open and honest and innocent as it could be. She was just fifteen years old.

She wouldn't get this.

But she was the one who begged you to go back to 92. The voice in her head screamed. She said she was broken and had secrets. Sky was the reason she was even here.

What kind of secrets could she have had that she had never wanted to be revealed?

Addi turned around and looked at her cousin fully. "What kind of secrets do you have?"

Sky laughed. She spun over on her belly and hit the bed.

"You are acting very weird." Sky finally finished laughing and then wiped her eyes. "I tell you everything."

"No, you don't." Addi frowned. "Tell me about Rusty."

"Rusty Brown?" Sky grimaced. "There is nothing to tell."

"Nothing?" Addi asked skeptically. "Nothing at all?"

"I like him, okay," Sky mumbled. "I mean I dream about tongue kissing him like they do on Dallas."

Addi snickered. "You do?"

"Yes." Sky wagged her finger at her, "and you are not to tell anyone."

"As if I would." Addi raised an eyebrow. "So, that's the big secret?"

"It's huge." Sky widened her eyes, "he is like old. He is twenty-two."

"Ah," Addi nodded.

"And he works for Dad and Uncle Nate."

"There is that." Addi nodded again.

"And he has a girlfriend," Sky muttered. "He lives with her. I hate that."

Addi glanced at her. She hadn't known that Rusty lived with his girlfriend when he killed Uncle Stan, just a mere two months from now in the old timeline. She couldn't remember anything much about his background except that he had a payment dispute with Uncle Stan and it got out of control.

"His girlfriend's name is Precious," Sky spat out the name, "and she is pregnant. That means they did it." Sky turned her woebegone face to Addi. "I wish it were me."

Addi swallowed almost choking in the process. She coughed and then spoke with difficulty. "What? Are you crazy?"

"Probably," Sky said. "We'd live together and he'd work for Daddy and Uncle Nate for a while..."

Addi snorted. "You are crazy!"

"Stop acting old, Addi," Sky said dreamily. "You have never heard Rusty sing. He sounds a hundred times better than Tevin Campbell. And do you realize he looks a little like him. He is just a lighter version?"

Addi wished she remembered details of how Rusty looked. Her last mental picture of him was that of a tall, slim, light-skinned guy with a goatee being handcuffed and shoved into a police car.

If she was going to prevent him from killing her uncle, it would be in her best interest to get to know more about this Rusty. And most of all she needed to convince Sky about her time traveling to accomplish this.

Addi looked at her cousin and contemplated how she would approach it. She had messed up her approach to Randy. She shouldn't have told him anything in the first place. She couldn't afford to mess up her approach with Sky.

She cleared her throat loudly.

Sky looked at her. "What?"

"I have to tell you something." Addi sighed. "I am not joking, okay? You need to take me seriously."

Sky raised herself on an elbow. "I am listening."

Addi frowned. Sky didn't look serious enough. She had a dreamy expression as if she hadn't quite gotten her head out of her Rusty world.

"Okay, let's go." Addi got up.

"We are going to look for Monica next door. You heard it from her once and believed her. You should hear it from her again."

"Monica?" Sky frowned. "You mean Miss Campbell? The lady that works at the bank? I have never spoken to her. What are you talking about, Addi?"

"Let's go." Addi got up. "I hope she is home."

"I heard she is kooky—has a screw missing." Sky sniffled getting off the bed. "She is an old lady who has issues."

"Forty is not old!" Addi looked at Sky in horror. "Aunt Ivy is forty-one, Mom is forty. I am..."

"Forty?" Sky chuckled. "Don't tell me you were going to say forty. And our mothers are ancient. Old school. Don't go defending them. What are we going to talk to Miss Campbell about?"

"You'll hear." Addi growled, pushing her cousin through the door.

Chapter Seven

Monica was on her way out when they trudged up the driveway. She was dressed in her bank uniform. A briefcase was at her feet. Her hair was jet-black, and her face younger than she remembered.

Addi closed her eyes and then opened them and stared at Monica. Twenty-five years in a couple of days. Time traveling had its disorienting moments. Addi stopped and stared at her for so long that Sky had to end up pulling her up further to the veranda.

"Why are you staring at her like that?" Sky muttered from the side of her mouth.

"She looks so young and sophisticated," Addi whispered back.

Sky snorted. "You need your head examined, ASAP. She's an oldie like the parents."

"Hello Ladies," Monica smiled at them. "How are you?"

"We are fine," Addi quickly said. "I was hoping you had a

moment to talk to us."

"Sure, anything for the Porter girls. You won't remember this, but I used to babysit Sky back in the days." Monica smiled, "come on in."

She pointed to the chairs on the veranda.

They sat down.

Addi cleared her throat and decided just to get along with it; she had already done the stammering bit with Monica. "I am a resetter."

Monica who had just sat down across from them froze. She looked at Addi as if she hadn't heard right. "Say that again?"

"I am a resetter. I was here two days ago, in 2017, talking to you. You told me that your grandmother was a resetter and that resetters had to make contact with pathways and then think about the date they wanted to go to and then they would appear there in their old bodies with their consciousness of their past lives intact."

Sky gasped and started coughing. Addi ignored her.

Monica had a wide smile on her face. "You dear girl. How extraordinary, apart from grammy I have never met a resetter!"

Addi exhaled. "So you believe me?"

"Of course," Monica said eagerly, "What is 2017 like?"

"The world is still spinning." Addi sighed, "I don't want to spoil it for you."

"Please don't." Monica grinned, "unless of course, I have a medical problem I can avoid or..."

"You looked fine to me." Addi sighed. "However, you did ask me to warn you off marrying Walter Sparks. He is not straight. You wasted five years of your life with him. Oh, and you want to have a child. Apparently twenty-five years from now you are broody."

Monica laughed and clapped her hands. "Husband? I

married Walter Sparks? Imagine that. Gay? You sure?"

"That's what you said." Addi shrugged. "I have no idea who he is."

"Thank you for the warning," Monica said somberly. "Thank you so much."

Addi nodded. "You are welcome."

Sky jabbed Addi in the side. "What are you talking about? What is a resetter?"

"I'll tell you later," Addi said and then turned to Monica. "You told me that you'd give me your grandmother's diary. Your brother cleared out the room where it was and destroyed it in 2005."

"He did?" Monica frowned. "Well then, I will give it to you as soon as I get back from work. Thank you so much, Addison."

Addi stood up. "You are welcome."

She and Sky headed down the drive together. Sky was giving her suspicious glances. "You ready to tell me about all the nonsense you just talked about with Miss Campbell?"

"Yes." Addi inhaled deeply and stopped.

"Go on," Sky urged when Addi was trying to put her thoughts together.

"Remember when you saw me yesterday morning at the rock?"

"Yep." Sky nodded. "You were acting strangely."

"The rock is a pathway."

"A pathway," Sky repeated. "A pathway to what?"

"The past." Addi cleared her throat. "I was in 2017, and I thought about coming back here, and here I am."

Sky looked confused. "Explain."

They sat on the wall at the entrance to the houses while Addi again tried to explain to Sky what was going on. It took her the better part of an hour to explain it again. Sky was equal parts astonished and equal parts unbelieving.

"You are telling me you are coming from a time that is further than Back to the Future 2, where Marty McFly went to the future?"

"Yes," Addi said with a sigh. "What time was it again? I haven't seen that show in so long. It's a bit of a classic in 2017."

"They went to October 2015," Sky said her voice faint, "Were there flying cars?"

"No," Addi muttered.

"Self-tying shoelaces?"

"Yes but not popular or anything." Addi frowned. "I really need to see that film again."

"So what was I like in 2017?" Sky asked. "Was I married to Rusty?"

Addi inhaled noisily. "No, you weren't."

Uncle Stan drove up to the house, and he wound down his window. "Addi, Sky."

"Hello Uncle Stan."

"Hi Dad," Sky said.

"How was the exam?" He asked Sky.

Addi didn't listen to their conversation. She just watched her uncle in awe. He was the lighter skinned version of her father—same features. They were obviously brothers, could be twins. Uncle Stan was beefier though and his cheeks fuller, but the resemblance was stark.

Another thing she had forgotten through the years. Most of the pictures of him were old and faded. After the first year of missing him terribly in 93, the memories had slowly dulled at the edges.

He had faded in her mind's eye. Twenty-five years was a long time to remember somebody sharply, but here he was, alive and in living color. He was a ruggedly handsome man who always had on a ready smile.

He had loved Sky to the point of spoiling her. For Addi and Josh he had felt like a second dad.

How could she have forgotten that?

Uncle Stan was the one who would religiously take her and Sky to the ice cream parlor on Ward Avenue every Sunday, and then he would drive them around and show them the houses that the Porter Brothers had built. Then he would tell them funny stories and listen to them if they had problems and offer solutions.

Addi felt a deep ache in her chest as she watched him. It was inexplicably good to see him again.

He tooted and drove towards his garage.

Addi's eyes welled up with tears. Tears she knew she didn't want Sky to see.

"What's wrong?" Sky asked coming to stand in front of her.

"Nothing." Addi sniffed. "I was just thinking."

Sky looked at her suspiciously. "What's my dad doing in 2017?"

Addi sighed. "I need to give you your book."

"Which book?"

"You sent me back with a book addressed to you." Addi sighed, "I don't know what's in it."

Sky scratched her earlobe and then shook her head. "I don't think I want to hear anything else about the future for today, Addi."

Addi looked at Sky in surprise. "What?"

"I have a funny feeling, here." She pointed to her stomach. "This is too much information to be dumping on me."

Sky inhaled. "Just give me till next week. I don't know if I believe any of this future stuff. If you are not playing with me and you really know the future that means you know what's going to happen next. It's not like a mystery for you is it?"

"No," Addi said frankly. "And all of that shouldn't matter. What matters is that we need to move on this quickly."

"But this means you are not really my Addi, are you?" Sky asked her voice quivering. "You are like an older Addi trapped in my present cousins' body, like an alien."

"I wouldn't exactly call it trapped." Addi was getting annoyed. "And you are the one who convinced me to come back. You are the one who had some big secret in 92 that I had to help you with. You are the one that killed herself and...."

Sky gasped. "What? I would never do that."

Addi grunted. "You did. Don't take too long to come to terms with this Sky. This summer is a huge deal for our family. The longer you take to get on board the more certain things will go down as it went before."

She stomped toward the veranda and almost crashed into Randy who was walking out of the house.

"I need to talk to you." He gritted out before she could move around him.

Addi stopped. "Why?"

"You know why!" Randy seethed. "My grandmother called today and told me about the scholarship."

Addi nodded. "Good. Congrats."

"Not good." Randy gritted out. "Not good. What you told me can't be real. Follow me to the office. Your mother is inside. She can't hear this conversation."

Addi walked behind him, but her legs couldn't keep up with his. He held the door opened to the office and waited as she walked by him.

"How do you know, what you know?" Randy asked her, his voice clipped.

"I told you," Addi said plopping herself down in one of the office chairs. She looked around the office. At both ends were desks with two ancient looking computers on both desks. Ancient to her recently traveled eyes but new for their time.

One belonged to her dad the other to her uncle. She remembered how proud they were to buy them. How rare it was to have personal computers in 92.

In the middle of the space was a bank of file drawers. Before each desk were chairs and a fairly large space between each. A potted palm stood near the opened louver window where she could clearly see the blue rock in the distance.

The window to the back of the office clearly showed her, Mr. Jones, their neighbor wrangling with a car. He looked like he was knocking out a dent at the side of the thing or was he creating one?

She refocused on Randy who was leaning on the door his arms crossed. "Addison. Please. I need to know. Are you clairvoyant? Some kind of witch?"

Addi chuckled and flung her leg over one handle of the chair. "If I were fifteen, clairvoyant might be a word that I would have to look up."

"If you were fifteen?" Randall groaned. "So we are back to that?"

He moved away from the door and ventured further into the room. He sat heavily in the seat at the desk and looked at her sternly. "You will tell me now, Addi, how you know, what you know."

Addi laughed. "The stern voice thing does not work on fifteen-year olds, Randy. I have found through the years that teenagers on a whole don't respond well to barked orders"

Randy sighed and leaned back in his chair.

"You know what I used to do the first time I was in 92?"

Addi said contemplatively, "I would to sit over at Uncle Stan's desk and play computer games, like Tetris and Gobman and Pacman. You and I had a best score competition going and sometimes we would listen to the radio. JBC radio for Quench Aid Guess the Riddle and RJR for the Guess The Song competition.

"You know that JBC radio is no longer around? Come to think of it, JBC TV is no longer around either. It is called TVJ.

"Now Jamaica has one TV station and only five radio stations. In the twenty-first century it has over twenty radio stations, and as for TV, there are so many local channels. The last time I came here from America, I was shocked to see how many there were. Though, why I should be shocked, I have no idea."

She got up and headed for Uncle Stan's computer. She pressed the power button and it came to life with a whirring, beeping sound. She looked up at Randy. He hadn't said a word through all of her ramblings.

He had an incredulous expression on his face.

"Computers get smaller." She sat before the computer and swung in the chair. "Very small, like palm-sized small.

"Technology takes off grandly. You remember the words Microsoft and Apple. They will be big names in the computer industry. Telephones get smaller too and they are wireless. No more telephone booths at street corners. I don't really remember when the cell phone explosion began..."

Randy hadn't spoken. He was squinting at her contemplatively.

"The truth about 92 before is that, I was just living my life. I was so self-absorbed. I had no idea of world events or changes around me. I mean only a few fifteen-year olds do, right?

"I think for the majority of us we just live our lives. We live the small picture. We do our best. We struggle along with our lot in life, we make choices and decisions that are sometimes wrong and sometimes we get it right. For some things we cross our fingers consult a higher power, follow our heart, and we hope it will be all right in the end.

"For some of us, it never really is. For some of us, we might be better off in terms of material possessions, but at the end of the day when it comes to people and relationships we are stuck."

Randy was twisting his thumbs around. He dragged his eyes from hers and then looked at the desk.

There was only the silence of the machine as it finally started up. Her MacBook would have started a long time ago.

Randy leaned back in the chair, his hand over his eyes. "Addison."

"Yes Randall," Addi said raising her eyebrows at him.

He sat up straighter in his chair and looked at her. "That's enough storytelling for the day."

Addi grimaced. The skeptic hadn't died. "Okay. I hear ya."

Chapter Eight

The family went to church together that Sunday. She dressed in the most sophisticated outfit she could find in her teenie bop closet. An all-black, simply cut, simply designed, lace dress, was one of five choices. It was a style that had made the rounds again in the 21st century.

She did a braid out on her long thick hair, and it looked good. It looked like a wig she once had. Good grief, her hair now was her wig goal in the future. Her parents did a double take when they saw her.

"See, you do not need to process that hair of yours," her mother said a thread of admiration in her voice.

"I hear you," Addi had responded. "You are right, Mom." She had bothered her mother for years to get it processed when she had entered high school.

Her mother had been prepared for an argument she opened her mouth and then closed it. "Well, then, it is good to know you have seen the light."

"The girl is growing up." Her father laughed, seeing the incredulous expression on her mother's face.

Randy entered the hall area at that time in a black suit and light blue shirt with a striped blue and red tie.

He told them good morning.

His eyes had lingered on her a bit though.

Sky turned away from him. Cursing herself for the unnecessary flutter that her heart made when he came into the room. Randy in a suit had always been impressive. That, unfortunately, was a fact of life.

His ever-present handsomeness was like an itch under her skin. She sat between him and Josh. Uncomfortably aware that his hand was brushing hers.

He glanced at her once or twice and then away again; a small smile crossed his face as if he knew he affected her in some way.

I will show him, Addi fumed. As soon as it is possible, she would be dating other people. She had to make a list of possible suitors. She had three long years to wait but she would definitely be over Randy. Her life was not going to take the same trajectory as it did before.

Their church was one of the oldest churches in parish of Manchester. St. Mark's, or The Mandeville Parish Church as it was called, was in the center of the town.

It looks the same as it does in 2017, Addi thought looking around the outside of the old building.

It certainly would be familiar to some runaway slaves in the past and even the English soldiers who were buried in the cemetery from the mid-nineteenth century.

She exited the car and inhaled the air. Very cool almost a bit too much. She walked to the set of graves at the side of the church and read the stones. It had always been a fascination of hers—reading the headstones on old graves.

The dates on the stones were unbelievably ancient. The church was founded in 1816, she remembered her aunt Ivy coming out for the 200th anniversary celebration in 2016.

Aunt Ivy had actually just returned from Jamaica when Sky had dramatically killed herself.

She rubbed her hand across one of the graves and wondered if any of the people, now long dead had been resetters.

She wondered how they handled going back. How did they handle living their lives already and then going back to the past to change things? Who would believe such a thing?

She sighed. But how could you change lives if no one believed?

She felt a tremendous burden on her heart for the many things she would have to do this summer of '92 with no help whatsoever.

Sky was avoiding her like the plague.

She could understand Randy doing it. She had gone philosophical with him. Their very first conversation she had told him that they had been lovers. He had good reason to believe that she was crazy, but not Sky.

Sky was her partner in crime. The chief instigator of all things ridiculous. The reason she had come back here for heaven's sakes.

She turned away from the graves and her eyes met Randy's.

She wondered what he was thinking. He was standing at the door waiting for her.

"Your brother said that gravestones were your thing. A witch trait perhaps?" He smiled at her when she approached him.

"Yes," she nodded. "Aren't you going inside?"

"Sure. Just waiting for the most colorful and imaginative girl I know to stop caressing the old stones so I can escort her inside."

Addi squinted at him. "You don't know that many girls then."

Randy chuckled.

Sky went to sit with her parents. Both parents sat in the same aisle. Uncle Stan sat at one end, her dad sat at another. Their wives and children sat between them. Usually, she and Sky would sit together, but not this particular Sunday— Sky sat between her parents, as if she was ensuring that Addi had no access to her.

She held her head straight throughout the service.

Addi couldn't remember a word of what the Reverend preached. She was sure she had heard it all before anyway, she was too busy glancing over at Sky trying to catch her eye but to no avail.

Aunt Ivy kept looking between Addi and Sky, her brows puckered in puzzlement. It wasn't unusual for her and Sky to have disagreements and supposedly malice each other for days, but the family usually let them work it out.

So, after a while Aunt Ivy, ignored her trying to catch Sky's eyes and gave a small shake of her head.

Addi sighed. Her cousin was acting crazy.

"That's a big sigh," Josh whispered to her.

"That's because Sky is acting weird," Addi whispered back.

"You are the one that is acting weird these past couple of days," Josh replied from the corner of his mouth. "I don't know what's wrong with you. Yesterday Randy asked me if I think you are possessed."

"Possessed." Addi gasped and glanced over at Randy, "Possessed as in demons?"

"Yep," Josh murmured. "You've been telling him about having a past life and all sorts of nonsense."

Addi crouched down further in her seat. She had thought that she was getting through to Randy, at least a little. Apparently, she wasn't if he thought she was demon possessed.

She sighed again.

"Stop sighing." Josh pinched her and chuckled. "I don't think you are possessed or crazy. I know what's bothering you."

"You do?" Addi sat up straighter.

"Yup," Josh whispered. "It's obvious. You like him, and you don't know how to act around him. It's cute. But I warned him not to even think of entertaining this crush. You are my little sister, which means you are off limits. Way, way, way off. You are not to like any guy until you are twenty-five or so. Dad and I agreed that twenty-five is a good enough age for you to start dating."

Addi giggled and then clapped her hand over her mouth. Her mother was looking at her with a disapproving frown.

After the service they greeted the reverend at the door.

"You are looking lovely today Miss Addison." The reverend declared with a smile.

"Thank you, sir." Addi grinned. She had liked the Rev. He had been a truly godly man. He was a man who carried a burden for his parishioners and took his job seriously.

She wasn't surprised to see Monica at the front of the church in a light pink suit and a string of pearls. "Here you are Addi."

She handed four stacks of black diaries to her. "These were grammy's…handle with care."

"Thank you." Addi nodded. "I will take care of them. Maybe I will give them back to you in 2017."

"That would be lovely." Monica nodded. "I am happy that somebody else can read them and find joy in them. A fellow believer."

Addi nodded.

"About Walter Sparks," Monica whispered before Addi

could walk away. "He is a divorcee with three children. He likes me. He is a customer at the credit union where I work. We talk all the time and I thought that things were getting serious. Thank you from the bottom of my heart."

"No problem. You were the one that actually gave me that extra push to come back. How did your grandmother handle it?" Addi asked, "The resetting thing. Did anybody believe her when she went back?"

Monica patted Addi's shoulders. "She never reset anything. She owned the land with the blue stone. Sold it to your people years ago. She said it was a constant temptation. But every day she would go to the back of our property and look down at it, not in regret. Grammy didn't regret anything, but she needed to reassure herself that everything that happened in her life made her who she was. She liked things the way they were.

"When she was older, she contemplated it, but she never did go back. She always said this life was only worth living once."

Monica left Addi soon after that with what Addi thought of as both a rebuke and a truism.

A resetter who didn't believe in do-overs. Maybe because do-overs were trouble, and nothing was really accomplished anyway because no one believed.

****

"I am going to pick up Ellie." Josh pushed her half-opened door wider. She had been sitting and staring at Monica's grandmother's diary after they got in from church. She was feeling sort of reluctant to open them.

She looked up at Josh. "Okay. Have fun."

"We are going to Black River to pick up her little brother.

Want to come? You can get to meet her."

"Really?"

"Yes, really." Josh grinned. "I might take her back here for dinner too. Mom is doing fried chicken and glazed sweet potato. It smells good."

Addi sniffed the air. She could hear the sound of the chicken sizzling in the pot and the pungent aroma of deep-fried chicken. "It does smell good."

"Come on." Josh nodded at her.

"Should I change?" Addi looked down at herself. She had put on a black and white polka dot sundress earlier when she had come home. It was ridiculously short, reached her mid-thigh.

Josh looked her over. "No, you are fine, let's go."

She bounced off the bed. This was a great opportunity to meet Ellie. The first time around she had met her later in the summer. Maybe sometime in early August when Josh had actually started sleeping with her and had sneaked her in the house for an overnight stay.

She had woken up in the night and seen this strange girl in the bathroom. Things were already changing, and she hadn't yet done anything to intervene. She hadn't told Josh about his new ladylove yet.

She followed Josh through the living room.

Randy was sitting in there with her Dad, they were reading the Sunday Gleaner and commenting on news items.

"Going to Black River," Josh stopped at the doorway, "to do a favor for Ellie."

Her father grunted.

"Hey, where is that?" Randy piped up. "Can I come?"

Addi groaned.

Randy glanced at her and grinned. "I don't know this side of the island well, any opportunity I get to see new places, I am up for it."

"Sure, come on." Josh glanced at Addi.

"Addi will entertain us and tell us more about her previous life and freak you out."

Addi rolled her eyes and followed Josh to the car. She got into the back seat and Randy got in with her.

"I come in peace," he winked. "Doesn't make sense I go up front. Josh will soon be picking up Ellie."

Josh turned the car stereo to Power 106 and turned it down. He changed his mind when Whitney Houston's, All The Man That I Need came on.

"Love this." He looked back at Addi and grinned. "Hope Ellie will want to sing this to me one day."

He drove off and Addi rolled her eyes.

Randy watched her for a while, too long in her estimation.

She turned her face firmly to the window, watching the undulating farmlands flash by as Josh drove past.

All of this was built up into a large community in 2017. She felt like pointing out the area that Randy will build and live in her dream house, but she changed her mind.

Already things were changing. Maybe Randy and Kenya would not be a thing? Maybe he wouldn't be living here?

Why did that thought excite her? She glanced at Randy who was still looking at her a hint of laughter in his eyes.

"What year were you living in before you came back here at fifteen?"

She looked at him and growled. "2017."

Josh laughed. Hitting the steering wheel in mirth. "So, in your past life you were what, forty?"

"Yup. The big four-oh," she said sullenly. "Though I didn't actually get to see my fortieth birthday. Technically, I was thirty-nine."

Josh slowed to a crawl over a bad patch of road. "So what is

Whitney Houston doing in the future?" He asked, as another Whitney Houston song, Higher Love, started playing.

"She died in 2012," Addi said without pause. "In a bathtub, drug overdose."

"Stop it!" Josh was not taking her seriously. "I knew you didn't like Whitney. Why would you kill her off?"

"I like her songs." Addi smirked. "I do. I am just answering the question you asked. It's kind of ironic though, me knowing this. Some of her greatest hits aren't even out yet."

Randy cleared his throat. "Told you she was a witch."

Josh looked back at his sister. "So, what happens to Michael Jackson?"

"Dead too, 2009. Drugs. I think that one was doctor administered."

"And Kriss Kross. Your little boy group?" Josh kissed his teeth, hating her bleak report.

"Chris Kelly died of a drug overdose too. I mean the song Jump was their main hit. This year was really it for them."

"Boyz II Men," Randy joined in. "What happens to them?"

"They broke up." Addi shrugged. "I have no idea where any of them are, but I am sure they are still alive."

"Madonna," Josh said, speeding up over the bumpy road.

"Still alive and still doing shows."

"And TLC," Randy was warming up to what he was thinking was a joke.

"Left Eye died," Addi said, "car crash."

"Stop," Josh said. He looked visibly upset. "I don't think I want to hear anymore about your past made up life. All my favorite artistes are dead."

Addi pursed her lips. "But..."

"We haven't asked her about any local artistes yet." Randy protested. "She can't stop yet."

"But she is so morbid." Josh glanced in the rear-view

mirror at her, "and so specific, it's kind of scary."

Randy gave her a half smile. "I told you. This guess the future activity was kind of grim."

Addi inhaled. "Well then, I won't say another word."

"At least let us know what happened to Shabba Ranks and Ninja Man." Randy urged eagerly.

Too eagerly. Addi had a suspicion that he was half believing her but didn't want to admit it.

"And Papa San and Lt. Stitchie and Tiger." Josh was back on the future game bandwagon but not as enthusiastically as before.

Addi sighed. "They are all alive as far as I know. Shabba faded out of the spotlight, Ninja Man was in jail at one point. Papa San and Lt Stitchie became Christians and started doing gospel and Tiger was injured in a bike accident in 94. I remember that because we were preparing to leave Jamaica. Grandma filed for us to go to the States and it came through..."

She stopped talking. She didn't miss the look between Randy and Josh.

Josh slowed down then came to a complete stop beside a house with a huge lawn. The house was a sprawling edifice with a few heavily loaded orange trees. Ellie was waiting on the veranda. A stern-faced gentleman of indeterminate age was sitting on the veranda beside a plump, short lady with long wavy hair. Ellie seemed as if she had been arguing with them.

Ellie was a beauty. She had long curly hair, caramel complexion, natural red lips and the kind of breasts women paid big money to get. She had on a red tank top that looked like it was barely holding them together and a white shirt over it that was far from modest.

She was dressed in tight blue jeans that emphasized her

tiny waist and flared hips. She had the kind of shape that people stared at, and she knew it. She walked with come-hither sway that was probably as natural to her as breathing.

She had seductress written all over her. Addi felt like getting out of the car and buttoning up her white blouse all the way to her neck.

Randy and Josh had gone silent when they saw her. A silent male appreciation that had Addi gritting her teeth.

Josh roused himself from his inertia and got out of the car. "We are done with this game," He said to Addi. "No more, you hear me!"

"Sure." Addi growled. "I will not spook your new girlfriend."

Josh nodded, seeming to already forget her predictions. He was eager to meet Ellie's uncle and aunt, but Ellie was already walking to the car. She looked almost tearful, but she brightened when she came closer to Josh.

"My uncle is being crazy again," Ellie said sliding into the front seat. "My brother is just ten and he has no place to stay for the summer. My aunt whom he was staying with is leaving for a couple of weeks and my uncle doesn't want him to stay here in Mandeville. Poor Owen. I wish my parents would hurry up and send for him, so he can live with them in the States. He can't live like this—being boxed around to different family members like an unwanted piece of luggage.

"Sorry to vent, Josh. Thank you so much for helping me out, my uncle doesn't want Owen here, so he decided not to take me to get him. That's like cruelty, isn't it? Owen can't live alone without adult supervision."

She looked back at Addi and Randy. "Hi."

Josh carried out introductions and they nodded politely.

Ellie's problems were quickly put on the back burner as she started talking about something else.

She was so effervescent; it was easy to see why Josh was so fascinated. The girl was sex in heels and had a personality that put you at ease. Josh was a goner and it had barely been a week.

Randy rested his head on the seat and looked at Addi while Ellie and Josh got caught up in their own conversation.

"So are all of the popular artistes now dead in the future?" Randy brought up their previous conversation again.

"No." Addi shook her head.

"Tell me something else that will make me wake up tomorrow and be convinced that you are really a time traveler," Randy murmured lazily. "Something that will make me say, wow. She has to be!"

"I have done a pretty good job so far." Addi chuckled. "Your grandmother called. Your birthmark is where it always was. Your unbelief is tiring."

"World events," Randy said, "Tell me something."

"I don't remember much." Addi squinted and looked through the window. "92...92..."

"Your dad and I were discussing the US Elections. Your dad was speculating about who Bill Clinton would announce as his running mate."

Addi laughed. "Oh, that's easy, Al Gore. And he'll win too. His wife Hillary actually ran in 2016...Forget that. So if you hear that Al Gore is Bill Clinton's running mate you'll believe me?"

Randy looked at her for a long moment. "Reluctantly."

He lowered his voice. "There is no way you could have known about Freda and that mark on my butt without insider information. I am getting there, Addi."

Addi examined him closely his eyes were genuine, pure brown sugar eyes that looked as if they had a light at the back of it. Eyes that were as mesmerizing now as they were in the future.

She bit her lip and then dragged her eyes from his. "That's a start."

"You are pretty," Randy murmured in surprise as if he was just seeing her for the first time. "And different. And you do act and talk much older than your age."

Addi smiled. "Thanks, I guess."

"One day, you'll have to tell me about us. I mean your future version," he said it quietly and then looked away from her.

****

She headed straight for the kitchen when they got back from Black River. The place smelled really good. She had to stop for a brief moment and inhale the air. Fried chicken with paprika and glazed sweet potatoes, oh the scent of it. It was the definition of a nostalgic childhood scent, anywhere she went, and she got the hint of this scent it would bring her back to her childhood and here she was inhaling it in 1992.

She entered the kitchen further, there was an orange bundt cake cooling on a rack on the counter. She couldn't remember the last time she had orange cake.

"You guys back already?" her mother was setting the table.

"Yes," Addi whispered, "Josh's girl and her brother are here."

Vicky smiled. "Well, we have enough food."

"Don't you think it is ridiculous how quickly he is taking her here to meet the family?" Addi asked urgently. "He is getting too serious, too quickly. You should see him when he is around her. He is like a lovesick puppy."

Vicky looked up at Addi and frowned. "It's just dinner."

"That's where it starts." Addi moved closer to her mother.

Knowing that this was a long shot. Her parents liked everybody.

They were neutral on all their friends. She could not in all her life remember either parent saying anything negative about anybody. Even after the whole Ellie debacle with Josh they hadn't said a bad word about Ellie though she deserved it.

Her mother stopped fixing the table. Put her hand akimbo and glared at Addi.

"You are to be hospitable and nice to Ellie and her brother, what's his name again?"

"Owen," Addi said reluctantly. The little boy had not said a word on their way from Black River. He looked unhappy and withdrawn, which made her feel bad for him, but he was beside the point. His sister was the evil Ellie—the woman who derailed her brother's life.

Her mother passed her and walked to the stove. "You are going to be hospitable and the sweet girl we know you are Addison Porter."

Addi felt like stomping her foot when a feeling of impotence assailed her. History was going to repeat itself. She couldn't very well blurt out to her mother that she was a time traveler and knew how all of this was going to end.

Though to be honest none of this happened before. She had never met Owen, nor had Ellie ever come to Sunday dinner. Maybe meeting the family had changed Ellie from a two-timing hussy who tricked her brother into marrying her and accepting another man's child as his.

Fat chance of that happening.

She left the kitchen and headed to her room. She didn't want to hear about how hospitable she should be to Ellie. She didn't want to watch the introductions to the parents either. Her parents would love her. Ellie had genuineness about her that even Addi after knowing what she did, loved. It would be like hating a kitten. You know you are a monster if you hate kittens.

She sat on the bed with her chin in her hand. If she blurted out at dinner that she knew what Ellie did, she was going to be in big trouble.

Firstly, because it had not happened yet and secondly, it would be the heights of being impolite. Her parents would punish her. She hadn't gotten a spanking since she was twelve, she didn't want them to rethink that mode of discipline now. It would be undignified.

Her brother would probably never speak to her again and Randy...maybe Randy would help. He did say he was slowly becoming a believer.

But if he took her side when everyone else thought she was crazy. His summer here would probably be terminated early.

She inhaled and stood up. She had no plan. Not even a ghost of a plan. She needed one and fast.

Chapter Nine

Her mother gave her a sharp warning look when she sat the dining room table with the rest of the family. It was a clear message to behave herself, one which she would gladly heed. Being the sullen quiet sister was not going to accomplish what she wanted.

Ellie was seated to her left, Randy to her right and Josh was seated beside Ellie on the other side of the table. He was grinning from ear to ear like the cat that got the cream, spoiled cream, Addi corrected herself.

Her mother served the food buffet style, in their good China. The ones with the blue and red grape designs at the edge. She still had them in 2017. They were still only taken out for Sunday dinners.

She had threatened to leave them to Addi in her will. Addi dearly hoped not. She didn't have the same tastes in floral designs as her mom did.

"So Ellie," her mother was the first to open the conversation to Ellie when they had all taken their share of food. "Tell us about you. Up until now we only knew that you were drop dead gorgeous and worked at Mack J's."

Ellie laughed. A tinkling sound. Infectious. She had the whole table laughing with her except her father. Addi noted. He was not even looking at Ellie directly. He was trying to hide it, but he wasn't pleased that Ellie was there.

Addi felt a little kick of elation. Her dad could be a potential ally in getting Josh to see Ellie differently.

"I go to the Culinary Training School," Ellie said in answer to Vicky's question. "The one on Ward Avenue. I hope to get certified and then move on to the training hotel in St. Ann. I want to be a chef."

"Ah," her father piped up. "That sounds good. My sister-in-law, Ivy Porter, is the principal of that school."

"Yes, I know." Ellie nodded. "I like Mrs. Porter. She sometimes teaches the advanced culinary classes. She is awesome. She does everything so effortlessly."

"So you are doing classes this summer?" Her mother asked. She was playing detective.

Addi relaxed somewhat. Her parents may be accepting and look unassuming, but they knew how to do their due diligence. To an extent.

"Yes." Ellie answered her question. "I go to classes in the mornings. Then I work at my uncle's place for the lunch and dinner crowd."

Her mother nodded and smiled. "So you are an industrious girl."

So much for due diligence, Addi almost groaned aloud. Her mother was positively brimming with acceptance. She could see the wheels turning in her mind, Ellie was responsible— she had a job and wouldn't be leaching after Josh. Ellie was pretty and warm and was quite the conversationalist. And the list would go on.

Addi almost missed Ellie's answer as she watched her mother fall under Ellie's spell.

"I have to be industrious." Ellie smiled, "my parents instilled a work ethic in me from day one. Besides, I have to help my little brother here with pocket money."

Addi looked at Owen when she said that.

The kid was as mousy and quiet as it was possible to be. She wished that she had known about him in the past. She wracked her brain trying to come up with even a hint of Ellie Dunn's family history. She was coming up with nothing. Owen wasn't around when Ellie and Josh got married. Not that she could remember.

All she knew of Ellie was that she was a pretty girl who Josh sneaked into the house at night. In August of 92 she had actually met her exiting the bathroom. Mid-August, Uncle Stan had died. Josh had gone back to university. Nobody really knew anything about Ellie. Everybody had been distracted and grieving. October in the last timeline she hadn't cared about Josh's love life.

He had come home one weekend in October excited about a scholarship offer to attend MIT, and then he had gone out Saturday night and returned subdued and sad looking. He had spent most of that month locked in his room.

Maybe that was when Ellie had told him of the pregnancy.

That November he had announced to them, at a Sunday dinner similar to this, that he was going to marry Ellie. The parents had been shocked. Addi could remember it now as clear as day. Her father had gone stone cold still. Her mother had looked like she had swallowed something distasteful.

"Why?" She had been the one to ask.

"Because she is pregnant," Josh had replied flatly.

Her mother had gasped her mouth hanging open like a fish.

"Pregnant!"

Josh had stared down at his plate like a prisoner about to be executed.

And then her father, the voice of reason. "You don't have to marry her, we can help her through the pregnancy. You take up your scholarship with MIT and we will help her. When you are done with school then you can think about marriage and all of that stuff."

Josh shook his head vigorously. "She is not well. Her uncle and aunt kicked her out of the house yesterday, she's staying with friends."

Her mother's sigh had been loud enough to shake the house. "Do you love this girl, Josh?"

"Yes!" Josh had nodded definitively. "Yes, I do! I really do, and I can't just sit around and watch her suffer as she carries my baby and not do the right thing. The right thing is to marry her and let us be a family. I can quit school for a semester, work at the store or even work with Dad since Uncle Stan is no longer around."

Her father had leaned back in his chair, a no-nonsense look on his face. "You are finishing college."

Josh nodded. "Yes sir."

"You should take that scholarship," he said again.

"I have to see how well Ellie is doing first," Josh had insisted. "I can't just leave her."

Both parents had gotten up from the table almost as if they had rehearsed it. She could hear her mother crying through her closed bedroom door that Sunday.

In the week, Josh had taken Ellie to the house for the first time to officially meet his family. It had been a tense, awkward meeting, quite unlike now.

Ellie had looked slimmer, almost emaciated, her cheekbones sunken, dark circles under her eyes. She had rushed to the bathroom every other second.

Her mother had burst into tears and was inconsolable. Her father had sat stiffly in the settee, making eye contact with no one.

After Nelson was born, tensions between the parents and Ellie had evened out somewhat. They had quietly paid all of Josh's bills and he had graduated university getting his first teaching job. Ellie had also returned to school. She left Nelson with her in-laws while she finished her culinary degree.

Life went on until Nelson had developed severe anemia. Josh had readily offered to donate his blood, but they weren't compatible.

She knew more about paternity testing than she should because of that situation. Ellie had Type B blood and Josh had type O blood and poor anemic Nelson had type AB blood.

The doctor had taken Josh aside and asked him if he knew who Nelson's biological father was because the situation was urgent.

She would never forget Josh's face when he came home that night. It was a few months before they left for the States. It had been a summer then too. Shattered, was the word to describe her brother.

Addi tuned in to the conversation going on around her. Josh didn't look shattered now. He was laughing and happy and completely relaxed, unaware of what was coming to him.

Addi lost her appetite though the fry chicken was some of the best her mother had done.

She glanced between him and Ellie. She felt like blurting out, "I know your blood type Ellie Dunn. It is B. My brother's is O, so while you are cheating on him, just remember that your kid's blood type might not be compatible with his."

She kept her mouth shut though and forced herself to eat.

Randy was looking at her puzzled when he saw her intense regard of Josh and Ellie. She tried to ignore him. But every time she moved her head in his direction, she felt his stare.

She wasn't surprised to hear him volunteer to help her wash up.

"What's the matter, Witch?" He asked her while she silently filled the sink with water and dunked the plates in the suds.

"Nothing." She bit her lip. "You wouldn't understand."

"Try me." Randy offered.

"You like Ellie?" Addi asked, not sure where the question came from. It was probably lurking somewhere in her subconscious. She had wondered at least once sometime in the other timeline.

"She is nice." Randy shrugged. "Pretty. Why?"

"You wouldn't sleep with her, would you?" Addi asked suspiciously.

"No." Randy squinted at her. "Are you saying that I slept with my best friend's girl in the future?"

"No. I don't know," Addi mumbled, really sorry that she had brought it up now. "It's just that in the future. She did sleep with someone and had his kid. It would be nice to know who it was. She never told Josh who it was. I think she was protecting that person. If you were the one who slept with her, don't, okay?"

Randy nodded solemnly. "Okay. But I have a pretty good moral compass and I am not even remotely attracted to her."

Addi grunted. She didn't want to mention anything about his moral compass.

Chapter Ten

The next week was full of changes from what she knew would happen in the original timeline. For one, Josh spent much more time with her this time. He volunteered to help her paint her room. On Monday he actually got her out of bed in the early morning. He came with sanding equipment and plastic to cover her furniture and helped her prep her walls for painting.

She mislaid Monica's grandmother's books under the plastic coverings and got distracted sorting through old family albums when she had all intention of reading up about resetters.

But the family album was quite an adventure in itself. She hadn't seen the albums in years. A few of the pictures were yellowed with age. She pulled out a picture of her and Sky when they were toddlers. They were sitting on the lap of Sky's mother. Aunt Ivy had her hair in a very high afro. She looked so much like a young Diana Ross. Especially around the eyes.

When she got bored of inspecting old photos, she went to see Sky. Surely Sky would have come around by now, but Sky had pointedly and spectacularly abandoned her.

"She is gone to Colleen's place to babysit for a few days," Aunt Ivy said when Addi walked over to her house at midday.

"But she didn't tell me she was going by her." Addi frowned. Colleen was Ivy's youngest sister; she lived in the same neighborhood, just several chains up the road from them.

Ivy shrugged. "She said she wanted a change of environment and I agreed. She's been walking around here like a mad person for the past couple of days. I don't know what to do with Skyler when she is bored and acting tetchy."

"She could have told me," Addi said sprawling out on the living room couch—a more sophisticated couch than theirs. Everything in Uncle Stan's and Aunt Ivy's place looked better than theirs.

The house layout was the same but that was where the similarities ended. Stan had put in crown molding in the ceilings. He had changed from the terrazzo tiles that were popular in the eighties when they built the house, to ceramic tiles.

It was much easier to clean.

Aunt Ivy was a decorating genius that was way ahead of her time.

While Vicky had fake flowers, figurines and crochet pieces, Ivy believed in clean lines and earth tone colors and real indoor potted plants in giant vases. The living room wouldn't look out of place in a luxurious mansion.

Addi hardly visited her Uncle's house because she hadn't wanted to break anything or sully the pristine floors. At her house she could do anything, but over here, she had to watch herself.

"Would you like some cake, Addison? You can take it over to your house…share it for supper." Aunt Ivy said, "I have a whole pineapple upside down cake…made it today at school."

Addi nodded eagerly. "Thanks, Aunt Ivy."

She had forgotten that one perk of having her aunt as principal at a culinary school. The same school that Ellie was attending. Something she hadn't even taken note of before.

She pointed out this new information to Ivy who nodded.

"I know Ellie, she has a talent for cooking. She is one of the brightest in the department."

"Josh is in love with her," Addi mentioned slyly wanting to hear her aunt's take on Ellie.

"Is that so?" Ivy raised one finely arched eyebrow in the air. "Well, he is a guy, and she's a pretty girl with very obvious feminine assets. I'd dare say quite a few gentlemen are attracted to her."

Ivy sat across from Addi and twisted her lips distastefully. "As a cook, there is no doubt that Ellie is quite good at what she does, but as a person, I am afraid to say she is little better than a…"

Her voice faded away. She wanted to say more but thought better of it. She used a classical misdirection method and fastened her gaze on Addi.

"How is it going with you, Addison? Everything okay?"

Addi sighed. Ivy wasn't going to make whatever it was that was disagreeable about Ellie, slip. If there was something to know about Ellie she wanted to know now. It was crucial that she knew.

"What did Sky tell you?" She would humor her aunt for a while, but the subject of Ellie was too important to ignore.

"Nothing. Well, she let it slip that you were acting weird."

"She is the one acting weird." Addi smoothed the settee beside her and avoided her aunt's sharp gaze.

Aunt Ivy had the eyes of a laser. She was what people would call a handsome woman. She wasn't exactly pretty but she was interesting to look at. She dressed really well and lavishly. And she always wore her pearls. The colors would change according to the outfit, but she was a pearl wearer and a tea drinker, who put the 'prim' in prim and proper.

Maybe it was her English upbringing. Addi thought ruefully. Ivy was a mixed raced woman with a white father and a black mother. She had spent half of her life, up to high school, in England.

She still had the accent. And she pronounced her words with exact precision. There was no shortening of names for her. Sky used to tease her that she sounded just like Geoffrey, the butler, from Fresh Prince of Belair. And Aunt Ivy had despaired that her only child sounded a little better than a gangster's moll.

"Well, I won't interfere in your little tiff with Skyler." Ivy finally said after a mounting silence.

It was a wonderful tactic to get confessions or to get people to talk; most people didn't like the silence and needed to fill the space. It was a basic counseling tactic. Addi looked at her aunt and wondered how long she had been using these tactics on them.

She almost laughed. She had done a course in counseling where she learnt the technique.

"Tell me about Ellie." She brought the conversation back to Ellie Dunn. Right where it should be in the first place. If she had any hope of resetting her brother's future, she needed to hear anything and everything about Ellie.

It was Ivy's time to avoid her gaze. "I do not know anything much about her... As a principal you hear things..."

"Like what?" Addi leaned forward.

"Like the fact that Ellie is... er... how should I put this, not in the best of positions at this time. Her parents are abroad. They left the children out here with family."

"I know," Addi nodded. "Yesterday we picked up her brother from his family members in Black River. He is spending the summer with Ellie and other family members up here."

"Her uncle and his wife do not have the best reputation as being charitable." Ivy sniffed. "I hear that she may be supplementing her income from other sources apart from her part-time job with her tight-fisted uncle."

"I picked that up from yesterday—that he was not very kind." Addi nodded. "But how is she supplementing her income?"

Ivy sighed and looked down at her hands. "It's not important. What I hear is just rumors. At least, I really hope so."

She looked up at Addi. "I heard that Ellie's uncle loves young girls a bit too much, one teacher is worried that he may like his own niece in a not so familial way."

"What?" Addi widened her eyes.

"I know." Ivy sighed. "I don't want to believe it."

"But if it is true, Ellie is in danger from her own uncle."

"She may be." Ivy smoothed down her skirt. "She's a nineteen-year-old girl. She can take care of herself. She is a very street-wise, survival savvy girl. I wouldn't shed any tears over her."

"But Aunt Ivy," Addi was shocked. "You can't just leave it like that."

"I can," Ivy said firmly. "I hear these stories every day, what am I to do about them? I didn't even hear this directly, another teacher told me."

Addi sunk back down in her chair. She had never known any of this about Ellie before and probably wouldn't have known if she hadn't come looking for Sky or got Aunt Ivy talking.

"I'll go and get you that cake." Ivy got up. "You liked the raspberry biscuits your grandmother sent from New York?"

"Yes," Addi said automatically, "they were okay."

"Well, I still have them." Ivy walked to the kitchen, "Skyler and Stanley hate them. You know I don't eat sugar."

She packed up Addi with a whole stack of treats. It was only when she was heading back to her house that she realized that Ivy had done it again. Misdirected her with the news of Ellie's uncle so that she didn't have to answer the question about how she thought Ellie was supplementing her income.

Her aunt was good, a master of misdirection. The uncle news was worrying though. Had Ellie been a victim of rape?

When she went over to her house and was packing out the goodies, Randy came into the kitchen.

"Is there a supermarket nearby?"

"No. Just my Aunt Ivy's bakings. Sky abandoned me quite unceremoniously and Aunt Ivy doesn't have anybody else to dump her goodies on."

"Ah," Randy licked his lips when she put down the glistening pineapple cake on the counter. "Can I get a piece of that?"

"Yes. Sure. Take what you want." Addi stood and watched him as he cut a piece of the cake and then devoured it like he was hungry.

"So what's new with you?" He asked her with a grin.

"Nothing." Addi shrugged. "I just learned something that I didn't know in the other time."

Randy frowned. "What?"

"Well, before this Josh and Ellie got married because she

was pregnant. The child turned out not to belong to Josh."

Randy folded his arms. "Good grief. Was that why you were cautioning me not to have sex with Ellie?"

"Yes." Addi nodded.

"I am still pissed that you think I might deal with Josh's girl. And now you are saying that I might be this not yet conceived child's real father."

"Well, I have to look at everybody!" Addi sighed. "I can't have this happening again. It nearly destroyed Josh. He had applied for a scholarship earlier this year and in October he heard back from MIT. He got in."

"I know about the scholarship. He said if he applied, he wasn't going to tell anyone. He'd just do it and hope for the best," Randy said it slowly.

"Well he got it, a full scholarship. He was expected to start in January, but Ellie was sick, and Josh chose to stay behind to support her. He married her in early December and gave up his shot at doing something that he had always wanted for a woman who quite possibly was stepping out on him at the same time she was with him."

Randy wasn't even nodding he was looking at her without moving.

"Addi..."

"Don't tell me that you don't believe me, and that time traveling isn't possible and that I am making up things. Just tell me, how are we going to find out who Ellie was having sex with, because that is what started the whole madness with Josh. She deliberately slept with him this summer so that he could marry her, and she could give that kid to him!"

Randy closed his eyes and then opened them. That was his only movement.

"Nelson was born the first week of April 93. April 6th to be exact. If my calculations are right, Addi rubbed her hand over her face, the great conception will take place in late July, early August."

"I remember Josh sneaking Ellie to sleep in before this in mid-August. We have just a few weeks to stop this, maybe days. Who knows who Ellie is sleeping with now, it could be anybody!"

Randy sighed. "I met you a week ago. You refuse to shake my hand because you want nothing to do with me because of a supposed affair we had in another life."

"Timeline," Addi muttered. "I prefer timeline. Another life sounds too reincarnation like."

Randy chuckled deeply. "Addi, you are incorrigible. You are so...so...unique."

Addi rolled her eyes and walked away. "Okay then, I think I am going to have to go this alone."

"Wait." Randy grabbed her hand and pulled her back.

She looked at where his hand rested on her arm. He didn't pull it away he drew her closer.

"Listen to me," he whispered fiercely, his dark eyes alight with fervor. "You are crazy, and fifteen. And my best friend's kid sister and I can't believe I am so..."

He let her go. "Addi, Addi, Addi. I can't be attracted to a fifteen-year-old girl. A crazy fifteen-year-old girl. You are just a child now, but I can tell you are going to be one spectacular woman when you get older."

Addi grinned. "I am a child now, but I have a forty year old mind."

Randy groaned and moved away from the counter. "Which would make me the younger man?"

Addi chuckled. "Yes, I am a cougar."

"A what?" He raised his eyebrows.

"Twenty-first-century term." Addi shrugged. "Older women dating younger men. There is a proliferation of that in the twenty-first century."

"Oh." Randy inhaled. "I have to go back to the office. I have a batch of invoices to sort out."

"Wait," Addi clasped her hands beseechingly. "When you find out that Bill Clinton's vice-presidential candidate is Al Gore will you at least help me to save Ellie from her uncle? And in turn save Josh from their marriage?"

Randy inhaled. "I don't know."

"There is no way I should know that," Addi said pleadingly. "It's not something that a teenage girl sitting in Jamaica could know. I have no inside links to Washington. The only way I would know this is if I heard it before."

Randy grunted.

"Oh, I know." Addi hit her head, "Can't believe I forgot this. Today is July 6th. July 6 is the day when my cousin Hilda gives birth to twins at Mandeville Hospital. Hilda is my mom's niece from her brother. Hilda will give birth today to a girl and a boy.

"But she will have complications and fall into a coma. My aunt and uncle will stop by at around seven o'clock this evening. My uncle will come by asking for prayers and my dad and mom will have all of us gathering in a circle and praying like crazy that Hilda doesn't die and that she wakes up from her coma."

Randy raised an eyebrow.

"She won't die," Addi said. "She woke up the next day and was discharged from hospital a week later. She went on to have two more children. I went to Nicky's wedding in 2016. She is the girl who is going to be born today. They named her Nicole and the son William."

Randy nodded. "Well then..."

"Well then, you'll believe me?" Addi asked earnestly.

"I don't know. Maybe," Randy said reluctantly. "If any of

this happens tonight. You'll have to tell me how what you are telling me is even possible."

He left the kitchen.

Addi breathed a sigh of relief. He was almost there. She jumped around the kitchen like the fifteen-year-old she was supposed to be. Seven o'clock tonight could not come soon enough for her. And then she would have to sort out how they were going to track Ellie Dunn's movements.

Chapter Eleven

Addi volunteered to cook dinner. She needed something to occupy her until the evening—just one week back in the past she was not so enthusiastic about her mother's cooking anymore.

The first night back she had struggled with the cabbage, the second night had been corned beef, the third night ground beef and macaroni, and then there had been one dish after another that she didn't want to revisit. Weekday meals had never showcased her mother's strongest cooking skills.

Besides, her palette had changed. Her mother had gotten much better at cooking than she was now. They had even taken a course together in early 2010 when her mother had decided to retire and wanted something to do.

She decided to do sweet and sour chicken, it was the one dish she was always complimented on in the future and she could do it with her eyes closed. In the middle of her preparations, her mother came into the kitchen a puzzled frown on her face.

"When did you learn how to cook this?" She opened pots sniffed each one and looked at her daughter. "You've been spending time with Ivy?"

"No, Mom. I was reading a cookbook, seemed easy enough."

Her mother nodded and sat in a chair looking off into space.

"You look worried," Addi said gently.

"Yes, I am. Hilda is in the hospital. They took her in this morning."

"She'll be fine," Addi said confidently.

"I know. God is in control." Her mother sighed and then looked over at her. "These last couple of days you feel different."

"Different how?" Addi asked trying not to act surprised that her mother had noticed that she was not the same.

She hadn't given her mother enough credit for being observant.

"I don't know," her mother said vaguely, "maybe I am just being fanciful. You feel older, more mature. Maybe it's the way you are wearing your hair now or maybe it's your speech. My little girl is growing up."

She got up and gave Addi a brief hug. "Don't grow up too fast though. I like all of your stages."

She squeezed Addi's hand and then exited the kitchen.

Her Dad and Uncle Stan came in through the back door shortly after that. Both of them dressed in hard hats and coveralls.

"Hey Addi." Uncle Stan greeted her. "I hope you don't mind if we have a private meeting in here now. Too many ears outside."

Addi nodded and looked through the window. There were a few men milling about. It was payday. Her father and uncle were whispering and pointing at a paper.

She smiled to herself. The two of them had always been close—best friends to the end. She winced at the thought. Uncle Stan's end was very close.

She stiffened when a new figure joined the others in front of the office. It was Rusty! She knew it was him.

He was tall, light-skinned and had curly hair. The goatee was just a starter, not the full one she remembered when he was hauled away by the police. He was wearing old cement splattered jeans and a white merino vest which showed off his slim but muscular arms.

She couldn't see where Sky found the appeal or that he looked like Tevin Campbell. Maybe if you squinted really hard you could see a little resemblance to Damian Junior Gong Marley, without the locks.

But Sky found some unseen appeal that lasted decades, even though Rusty had killed her dad and despite the fact that Rusty had been in jail.

He was twenty-two now. He wouldn't be eligible for parole until he was forty-six and even then, Sky had kept in touch with him.

Addi glanced at the pot to make sure that the rice was not in any danger of being burnt and then went back to the window. Her uncle and father were whispering about figures and were quietly arguing about a particular worker because he was on the site for just an hour.

She zoned out of their conversation and focused on Rusty. In precisely thirty-four days he would kill her uncle presumably because of a pay dispute. She had some time to stop that and she needed Sky's help. Maybe Sky had written something in that book marked for Sky Porter Eyes Only.

Addi sighed. So many things to do this summer. She had no idea fixing things would be so hard.

She gritted her teeth in frustration. It wasn't going to be easy manipulating lives or convincing people not to do certain things. And if she were not successful, she would be reliving her same old life again.

"That's a big sigh young lady." Uncle Stan looked up from the paper he was holding and grinned at her. "You okay?"

"Fine. Pondering the vagaries of life." She shrugged and turned away.

Her father and uncle looked at each other.

"Vagaries," her father mouthed to her uncle. "Where's the dictionary?"

She didn't see when the two men chuckled and headed to the back door.

****

They had dinner. Compliments abounded for her sweet and sour chicken dish. She found it ironic because everyone at the table had the same dish through the years in her past life and said nearly the same things.

Her mother was beaming proudly at her. Josh was going at his plate like he had not eaten since the morning.

Her father's comment had Randy looking sharply at her.

"This seems like a dish that you have perfected, Addi. It's just right. I can't believe that this is your first go at it."

Addi looked at Randy and winked just when the clock made the hour sound. A small low gong.

And then the sound of a car as it drove up into the yard and stopped.

"I wonder who is that?" Her mother had her fork midway to her mouth.

Addi looked at Randy and winked.

The time of reckoning was at hand.

****

Her Uncle Victor was her mother's twin brother. They

didn't look very much alike. Victor was shorter, had a broad face, and a dimple in his chin. He was more on the chubby side because he loved his food and made no apologies for it. He was even bigger in the future and quite healthy too.

He was currently married to Laura who loved to cook. She had always thought of them as very happy with each other. Except that in the future they were both married to other people. Addi couldn't quite remember what had broken them up or when they had even split.

Addi had not seen Laura for years until Nicky's wedding a few months before her journey back to Jamaica to spread Sky's ashes. Laura had a hip problem and had to be assisted to the front of the church to see her granddaughter get married.

Seeing her look so sprightly and young was almost a shocker. Time had indeed been unkind to Laura.

Right now, both of them looked worried sick. Hilda was their youngest at nineteen. They had forced her into one of those shotgun marriages when she got pregnant to save face in the neighborhood where they lived.

Byron, Hilda's husband was eighteen, but he was from a wealthy respectable family, which had lost most of their money in the local financial meltdown that started in 93. Byron's father had killed himself after his furniture company had gone belly up in 96. Hilda had left him that year, moving back home with her parents and taking the children, Nicky and William, because Byron had gotten violent.

She looked at her uncle and Laura now and almost had to stuff her fingers in her mouth not to blurt out their futures. They wouldn't believe her, and they had too much on their plates right now to receive that kind of bad news at this moment.

She bit her tongue and worried her lip. She knew too much. Being a resetter was a burden.

As expected, her uncle sighed, sat down in the settee and looked at them all his eyes wet.

"Hilda is in a coma. They are saying she might not make it."

"We should pray." Laura moaned. She was not handling the news well at all. Her mother who had answered the door and left them at the table urged them up.

"Come on. You heard the man. Prayers can move mountains. The Bible says that if you have faith as small as a mustard seed...come on people."

Addi looked at Randy, he had pushed away his plate and was avoiding eye contact with her. She couldn't even crow, I told you so.

Randy had gone reflective. She wondered what on earth he was thinking. His face was like a fortress, closed to her.

They had prayer. Her mother had prayed a fervent, heartfelt prayer. Her uncle and aunt stayed until late, finishing off her sweet and sour chicken, even eating the leftovers from their plates.

Tragedy seemed to open Uncle Victor's appetite.

Randy had disappeared to his room so she went to hers, but she couldn't sleep. Even when she heard the hall clock give the top of the hour sound again.

She glanced at her small clock on the dresser. It was saying one o'clock. She got up and headed to the living room.

The house was silent. She heard a dog bark in the distance. She snuggled into the settee and watched as the lights from Uncle Stan's house-made patterns on the veranda walls as it intersected the tree nearby. She didn't know how long she stared at the patterns. Willing herself to sleep.

She heard when Randy's door opened and when he headed for the kitchen. He turned on the kitchen light and then she heard him enter the fridge and then he had something to drink and then washed the cup.

He couldn't sleep either.

That was good to know.

He was exiting the kitchen when he saw her in the settee, he came over silently. He was wearing socks and his familiar heather gray tracksuit.

"Hi Witch." His voice was quiet in the room.

"Hi." She cleared her throat.

"So we are having one of our midnight chats again." He settled in the settee across from her and sighed audibly.

"Seems so," She said flippantly. "Do you believe me now?"

Randy took his time to answer. "If I say yes, I am crazy and if I say no, I am in denial." he shrugged. "I believe that you know stuff. Stuff you shouldn't know. How you know them is so crazy. It's so way out there. It's..." he inhaled, "what do you want me to help you with?"

Addi sat up in the settee a blast of hope hit her in the chest and squeezed. He believed her.

Randy believed her. She fought the urge to go over to him and hug him. It wouldn't be appropriate now. It might never be that way between them again. She was going to reset Randy out of her life.

She would find somebody else.

For now, she would stamp down her feelings for him. Bury them. They couldn't see the light of day because she forbid it.

Randy was just her brother's friend and she was going to have nothing to do with him this time around. He was going to be free to choose his future and she was never going to interfere.

"Hey, you are zoning out on me." He clipped his fingers.

"No. Sorry." She cleared her throat. "I was just thinking about something. I need help to find out who Ellie is seeing beside Josh. We need to let him know what kind of person she was before he gets involved."

Randy grunted. "Or we could just tell him to wear a rubber when he sleeps with her."

"Condoms can break," Addi hissed. "I am talking about total prevention here. No sex with Ellie. Kill it before she starts it."

"Are you sure that you have the correct version of events?" Randy whispered. "Suppose Josh started their sexual relationship? Maybe Ellie is not the sexual aggressor you seem to be describing. Your brother is no saint, Addi.

"Besides, have you thought this through? How are we going to even track who Ellie sleeps with? How are we to track her?"

"We could spend time with them," Addi whispered back." I could invite myself along to all of their alone time. You could distract Josh for me, so he doesn't spend time with her."

Randy chuckled. "It won't work. Josh picks her up from school in the evenings. Before he drops her home, he takes her out for ice cream or something. I don't know where he goes with her, he doesn't tell me. He is an adult male with the hots for this girl. No amount of intervention is going to keep him away from her."

"This whole thing is harder than I thought," Addi muttered. "Can we at least find a whole day when we can track her, see who she interacts with, like a detective kind of thing?"

Randy shrugged. "I don't know. Maybe. Your father and uncle are going to a work site in Negril for a couple of days next week."

"I remember that." Addi clipped her fingers. "They left for a whole week. It rained every single day they were away. I spent most of that time reading."

Randy nodded. "Well then, I am responsible for liaising with the guy they have on the site in Ingleside until they get back. I am to check in everyday, three times per day. I could take you with me, if your mom says yes. We could check up on Ellie for a couple of days at various times. That's the best I can do."

"But it's brilliant!" Addi was almost salivating at the thought.

"Goodnight Addi." Randy got up.

"Wait!" Addi said suddenly feeling bereft. She thought he would have a million questions for her about the future instead he seemed almost resigned.

"What is it?" Randy asked.

"So don't you want to know more about...everything?" Addi asked the question almost desperately. She didn't want the only person who believed her to leave. She had loads of interesting information to tell him.

"No, not really." Randy shook his head. "Not now. Now I need to sleep, and you should too. Even forty-year-old teenagers need their sleep."

He gave her a little salute and left.

But Addi couldn't settle down. Her brain was ticking overtime thinking about her previous life with Randy.

Randy, Randy, Randy...

She eventually rolled over on her back and stared up at the ceiling. Her first encounter with him was this summer and then she had seen him at Josh's hasty wedding in December. He had been best man at the wedding. She hadn't been able to keep her eyes off him. It had been her first sighting of him since summer and that December had just cemented in her mind after seeing him again that her summer crush had grown and hardened into something else.

She had made a stupid vow that she was only going to love

Randall Vassell forever. There would be no one else for her.

It wasn't hard to keep her vow. Maybe if Randy was not around so much in her sixteenth and seventeenth year. Maybe if he hadn't been so handsome and attentive and kind to her.

Whenever he came to spend weekends, which was quite frequently, since Josh had to return home often, Randy would return here, and he would spend the weekend with her parents because Josh didn't have the room at his new apartment.

Randy had always remembered to get her a gift. He had always remembered her birthdays and her exams and all sorts of things that not even her own family was as aware of. She had taken accounts in high school because he was good at it and business was his area. It had also given her an excuse to call him every day to help her with her homework.

He had always found the time to help her. Sometimes breaking dates with girls his age, girls she was rabidly jealous of. He never wanted to discuss them with her, always deflecting her questions, always trying to act as if his only interest in her was as his best friend's sister.

She always sensed it was more than that and she waited, just as she was sure he was waiting, for her to grow up, become mature, be old enough to know what her feelings were. He never said it, she just assumed.

Years later he had confirmed that her assumptions were right. He told her he had liked her almost immediately but suppressed it.

And then came 1995. Her eighteenth year. Randy's final year of university. The year she migrated from Jamaica with her parents. The year he met Kenya and her good father the Reverend P.N St. Claire entered the scene.

The year when she thought her life would fall apart.

Randy switched from business and went into ministry and

then by 1997 they were married.

She was trying to work out, which one was worse, 95 or 97.

She had spent most of 1997 and the days leading up to Randy's marriage in a miserable bubble. And nothing or no one could console her.

Addi closed her eyes tiredly.

This time around what would she like to have happen?

Change it all.

Forget about loving Randy.

Forget that you love him.

Forget that you love him.

Forget that you love him.

You'll be happier.

Would she really be? The question pounded in her mind until she drifted off to sleep.

Chapter Twelve

"**W**hat's wrong with your bed?" Her mother was standing over her, a cup of tea in her hands. She was in a shiny satiny taupe colored robe.

"It squeaks and is lumpy," Addi muttered, closing her eyes again. "It's a good thing my young back can deal with the torture. If I were your age, it would kill me. I'd wake up limping and maybe black and blue."

"Mmmph," Vicky muttered and then moved away, she heard rustling as she took her seat across from Addi. "We have had that bed for ages. Since Josh was born."

"No wonder," Addi muttered. Surprisingly, it hadn't bothered her the first time around because she hadn't known any better.

"I'll talk to Nate. We'll buy a new one by the end of the week. Something firmer."

Addi opened her eyes. "Thanks mom."

Vicky nodded and cupped the teacup in her hand. She looked thoughtful like she had a million and one things on her mind. The frown lines in her forehead got deeper the more she thought.

She finally focused on Addi.

"Your father and uncle are leaving for a couple of days next week. They need to finish up a project in Negril."

Addi nodded.

"I wanted to go to Kingston to visit a friend of mine who is in Jamaica for a while…spend two days but I can't go anymore. Nate wouldn't allow it."

"Why?" Addi asked eagerly. She couldn't remember this happening either. And what was even more surprising her father was not allowing it. She sat up straighter in the settee and wiped the sleep from her eyes

"I shouldn't go anyway not even with Nate," Vicky muttered. "Noel was my boyfriend before your dad. He is here for his mother's funeral."

Addi widened her eyes. She could not recall hearing about any boyfriends before her mother and father got married.

Their love story was solid. They met at university in their second year. They were each other's first, or so she had assumed. They had always been together, happy and well adjusted. In 2017 they celebrated forty-five years of marriage.

"Sometimes, you should let bygones be bygones." Vicky sighed and focused on Addi. "Some things should not be revisited."

"But sometimes you can change things, be at peace, set things straight, reorder them in the way they should have been in the first place." Addi countered.

"Yes, I suppose." Vicky sighed and then got up. She was obviously tired of the conversation. "You're painting today?"

"Yes." Addi stood up and stretched.

"Remember to wear a mask," Vicky said briskly, "and wear old clothes and do not mess up the furniture!"

"Yes ma'am." Addi headed for the plastic covered room and found the nattiest ugliest outfit that was in her drawer and pulled them on—acid washed jeans and a white t-shirt that was so stretched at the bottom it flared like a dress.

Her mother turned on the radio in the hall; as usual it was on RJR. The Good Morning Man show with Alan Magnus was on.

Somebody cranked up the volume. She could hear it through the door.

She had not listened to radio in years! She had a selection of inspirational and soothing music CD's in the car. She felt a real bout of nostalgia when she heard Alan Magnus' voice.

And then the familiar jingle, It's now time for Calypso Corner. Addi opened the door and went into the hall. Her father was there. He raised an eyebrow at her mode of dress.

"I am going to paint." Addi shrugged.

He nodded and then held up his finger when the calypso song came on. It was the song, Dolla Wine.

Cent, five cent, ten cent dolla. He started jerking his hips in tune to the music. Addi leaned on the wall and laughed.

Josh came out of his room at the same time and glanced at her and then his dad and shook his head.

"Dad loves his soca."

Addi nodded. She had forgotten that. She had also forgotten how playful he could be. Her mother came out of the kitchen to join him and they both danced enthusiastically to the music, while she and Josh watched them.

When the song ended her father grabbed her mother and kissed her at the side of the cheek. The two of them laughed and looked at their grinning children.

"And that lady and gentleman is how you keep young." Her father announced and then he looked at Addi. "Where are your painting supplies?"

"I don't know." Addi shrugged. "I was just about to ask you where I could get brushes and thinners and what not."

Josh chuckled. "Brush? That would take you all day. We are going to use rollers. Come on. Your supplies are in the garage."

****

Josh basically took over her painting project. He taped the corner edges of the walls. He mixed the paint. Randy joined them when they were moving the dresser out of the way and then he grabbed one of the rollers and she was left standing in the middle of the room while they made short work of her painting project.

When music from the Love Spot was announced on the Morning Man program. Usually, Alan Magnus played a love song that was positive and uplifting.

This morning was, I Just Called To Say I Love You by Stevie Wonder.

Josh looked at her. "Hey, future girl, what happened to Stevie Wonder?"

Addi glanced at Randy and then at Josh. "Still around. Still singing too. I went to a concert where he was one of the artistes. I went with Sky in 2016. Her last concert before she killed herself."

Josh laughed. "Ah boy, in your stories somebody has to die, eh?"

Randy didn't join in. He just continued painting, a grim look to his face.

"Why don't you ask me about you in the future?" Addi

asked testing the waters with Josh.

"Me?" Josh looked at her, "Well okay, what's happening with me. Please say I am still around. Unlike Sky and all of the singers you told me about."

"You are." Addi sniffed, "but you are unhappy."

Josh finished one side of the wall. "Why am I unhappy?"

"You got married to Ellie this year because she was..."

"Addi!" Randy was the one who turned to her and shook his head. "Stop."

"But he deserves to hear!" Addi wailed.

Josh looked between her and Randy. "I deserve to hear what?"

Addi swallowed. "Ellie is not the person you think she is. She did something very bad to you in the future. I think she is cheating on you now."

Josh froze. "That is not funny," He finally said. "This joke, this future thing. Ends now. You hear!"

Addi nodded and swallowed. Josh looked livid. She could see his Adam's apple bobbing up and down as he stared at the wall, holding himself rigid.

"Don't ever say anything about Ellie ever again. You hear me?"

She nodded again.

He finished his side of the wall in silence.

Randy gave her a look. It was as if he was saying, I warned you. Serve you right.

But telling Josh was worth the try. She kind of felt deflated about how vehemently he had shut her down. But a small spark of happiness blossomed in her chest. At least Randy believed her, as preposterous and crazy as her story was. Randy believed her still. She had one ally in this summer do-over.

****

Addi spent most of the rest of the day feeling restless. Her room was painted. Very neatly at that. It looked bigger too because of the lighter color they used. She placed a pan with water in the middle of the room to absorb the scent and then left the door wide open.

The day was overcast and very cool, bordering on cold. She used some of her pent-up energy to walk to Uncle Stan's house. She needed to talk to Sky, but Sky had not returned from her self-exile at Colleen's house. Nobody was home. She contemplated going to the office to spar with Randy but thought better of it. He hadn't looked too pleased after her impromptu revelations to Josh.

She decided to take a stroll around the neighborhood instead. The guava trees across from the houses were loaded. She took off her sweatshirt and made a makeshift bag to carry home some of the ripest and biggest ones.

Mrs. Jones, their neighbor waved to her when she was heading back.

Addi waved. She didn't remember what Mrs. Jones first name was. She was standing at the front step of her house just staring into space. She looked quite young too. Maybe early thirties.

She had a square face, and thick eyebrows that were neatly shaped and an almond nut complexion free of blemishes. She was surprisingly slim now.

In all of her recollections of Mrs. Jones she had never thought of her as young looking or even beautiful.

She had concluded maybe upon seeing her once or twice that she was just drawn and burdened and perpetually pregnant.

"Do you want some of my guavas?" Addi decided to make an overture. She could not recall ever talking to this lady though they lived beside each other for years. That had been one of her regrets.

It was time to reset.

"Thank you." Mrs. Jones nodded. She went for a container and Addi dumped the guavas in them.

She shook out her sweater and tied it around her waist.

"I can make jam." Mrs. Jones smiled. "Thank you."

Addi smiled back. "It's nothing. They were falling from the tree in the common over there. You know, I always thought that jam was hard to make but found out that it was pretty easy a couple of years ago."

"A couple years ago?"

Addi groaned out loud. She had been getting her mouth in it from morning.

"You are one of the Porter girls aren't you?" Mrs. Jones asked.

"Yes." Addi nodded. "I am Nate Porter's daughter, Addison."

"I am Myrna Weir."

"Myrna Weir? As in you are not Mrs. Jones?"

"No." Myrna laughed. "I am not married to Keith. People assume we are, so I just answer to Mrs. Jones. It's easier, more respectable. Maybe one day we'll get married."

"I always thought you were married." Addi gaped at her. "Whenever, I see you, I think Mrs. Jones who is always pregnant..."

She clapped her hand over her mouth.

Myrna laughed. "Not always. I have just five children."

"Seemed like more." Addi mumbled feeling embarrassed. "Where are they?"

"They are spending summer with Keith's mother. I was standing out here thinking about them. The house seems empty without them."

Addi nodded. "I hear my friends who are mothers say that

all the time."

Myrna glanced at her sharply. "How old are you?"

"Old enough," Addi said, flippantly sitting on the step.

Myrna found her funny. She laughed. "Well then, I am thirty this year."

"Just thirty." Addi shook her head. "That's too young to be so discontented."

Myrna sighed and sat beside her. Still with that thoughtful look on her face. "When the children are here, I am distracted by all the noise and the motherly stuff. When they are gone, I wonder..."

She sat back on her hands and looked out. "I wonder if I am not wasting myself here with Keith and..."

She stopped speaking as if realizing that Addi was up to now a stranger.

Addi waited for her to weigh the pros and cons of speaking about it. She wasn't going to prompt her.

"I wish I had money," Myrna finally said. "I would buy a sewing machine. That's my skill you know. Sewing. My aunt did it and I used to help. She did drapes and curtains and spreads and those kinds of things. I was really good at it too. I could do it again. I need to do something. This inactivity is killing me."

Addi glanced at her. "My mother has a sewing machine that she hasn't touched for ages. I could ask her to lend it to you."

Myrna clasped her hands in front of her and then looked at Addi. "Really?"

"Yes, why not?" You'll need other stuff too, like a cutting table and sewing stuff.

Myrna looked deflated again.

"Tell you what," Addi got up and brushed herself off. "I need a new bedspread and pillowcases and matching curtains.

You do my stuff for free and I can get you everything else you want."

"How?" Myrna frowned. "You are just a kid. A nice one but..."

"I'll do it." Addi held out her hand. "Deal?"

"Deal." Myrna took her hands slowly.

****

Addi headed straight for the office when she entered the yard. Randy had a large ledger in front of him and a calculator punching numbers into. He didn't even look up when she entered the office.

He was whispering numbers under his breath and jotting figures down on a piece of paper.

He finally looked up. "Yes, Addison Porter."

"I want to help Myrna from next door to get a sewing business started."

Randy nodded. "And how may I assist you in this?"

"You can tell me how a fifteen-year-old in 1992 can make money quickly and legally."

Randy sighed and closed his eyes. "Addi..."

"Yes Randy," she leaned forward and grinned. "You do long-suffering so well."

Randy grimaced. "How did I become your sidekick?"

"Because you are the only one who believes me."

"And for that, I should have my head examined." Randy tapped his pen on the desk. "To make money legally you can always try horse racing. There is a shop in every major town."

"I have no idea about any horses." Addi sighed. "I don't even know what the interior of one of those places look like. I always found the whole horse racing thing boring."

"Well, there is the informal betting at Chung's Haberdashery. They bet on everything. Sometimes, the stakes are pretty high, like half a million dollars."

Addi nodded slowly. "What can you bet on?"

"Like presidential elections, celebrity stuff both local and international, the Summer Olympics in Barcelona this year, other random stuff. Everyday there is something. Your Uncle Stan told me that he made a killing from predicting who would succeed Michael Manley when he stepped down as prime minister this year."

"My uncle doesn't gamble," Addi muttered.

"Look at that, she doesn't know everything!" Randy laughed and hit the desk. "What, in the future he has no vices?"

Addi leaned back in the chair. "In the future he is not around."

Randy went silent. "Oh Addi."

"We have to save him too." Addi whispered, "but first, we need to work on getting some money."

"I don't gamble either." Randy tapped the desk. "But I am going to go out on a limb here and justify this okay?"

"Okay." Addi watched him closely. Today he was looking especially handsome. His face was closely shaven, his dark brown eyes sparkling, his pink lips firm yet soft.

She could remember every time they had ever kissed, including their first kiss, when he had shown up at her off-campus apartment and begged her not to let him inside.

"If you know the future it's really not gambling is it?"

"Huh?" Addi dragged her mind from the future that would never be and into the here and now.

"Gambling," Randy repeated patiently. "For you, this is not gambling."

"True." Addi nodded. "Which makes life totally boring

and no fun. Not knowing the future is actually half of the fun of living."

Randy smirked. "Well...you would know."

"It is so." Addi grunted. "So what are we going to bet on?"

"You are going to bet on the upcoming presidential pick for US vice president. It's two days away. Your uncle told me about it." Randy pointed at her. "You'd better be right because I am giving you all my savings."

"Randy you are the best!"

"Remember to tell me this, when you are an adult. Now scat, I need to give this estimate to your father and uncle by this evening."

Addi left the office beaming.

Chapter Thirteen

Addi did her usual stint in the settee, this time because the fumes from the freshly painted walls were too much for her. She found Monica's grandmother's diaries under the bed of all places and had already read through the first one.

She was a good writer. Very engaging. She wrote about her life like a story, Addi appreciated that. The first diary had her hooked. She started reading:

My name is Gwendolyn Fisher, and I was born on October fifth, 1921, to Perkins Fisher a wealthy landowner and citrus farmer and Theresa Fisher, housewife. I was the third of seven children, the only girl. It was my grandmother Dorothy Fisher who first recognized that I had only two lines in my palms. She was considered superstitious, and no one took her observations seriously so this out of place phenomena was discounted. Jamaica in the twenties was a place of change...

Addi read through what she was loosely calling in her head book 1. Her concentration was so engaged in the book. She jumped when a hand tickled the soles of her feet.

"Wha?"

Her father was holding a glass of water and grinning. "I said, what are you reading Addi?"

"I didn't hear." Addi grinned at him. "It's good stuff. A diary from Miss Monica's grandmother, Gwendolyn Fisher Campbell."

"Ah, Miss Gwen." Nate sat down across from her and sipped his water.

"What's wrong?" Addi frowned at him and then looked at the clock. It was a little after midnight.

"Heartburn," he said closing his eyes and leaning back in the settee. "Vicky said I should sip some water and baking soda slowly. Remind me never to eat tomatoes again."

"Tomatoes." Addi grinned, so that's why he never touched them in the future. "Yes sure."

"You should go to bed," he said taking another sip of his water.

"I can't, my room smells awful, and I hate my bed."

"Right." Nate closed his eyes. "Your mom told me about the bed, and I can smell the paint from out here."

"Dad, tell me about Miss Gwen." Addi closed the book. She was almost done anyway. Miss Gwen had a lot of stories about her early life but nothing about the two lines in her hand.

"She was a lovely old lady," Nate said softly, "very good with names and history. She was like a walking herbal encyclopedia. I think she was a genius or something. You just needed to point at a plant. She could tell you the scientific name and its uses and all of that stuff."

Addi nodded. "In her diary, she said her father owned most of the property around here when she was younger."

"Yes." Nate nodded. "He left chunks of it to all of his

children. Miss Gwen had owned this side of the land for miles around. But she sold it out through the years. When Stan and I were looking around for a place to build we heard about her and how reasonable she was selling the property. We drove all the way from Mile Gully where we were living at the time to see Miss Gwen. It was a Sunday, Miss Gwen had just come from church, and we had you and Sky with us. We drove up the long driveway up to her house.

"She heard us out as we politely enquired about land and said, 'I am so sorry gentlemen I have nothing available for sale.' And then you came out of the car. You were just five at the time."

Nate chuckled. "You were super cute too. You came out saying, 'Daddy Daddy I want to go potty.'"

"Miss Gwen offered to take you to the bathroom. When she came back with you, she practically gave us this piece of land. To this day Stan and I have no idea what made the difference."

My palms! Addi subsided in the chair. Miss Gwen must have seen my palms and known that I had the same resetting abilities.

It was uncanny she didn't remember that episode with Miss Gwen. It was also funny that her father had never mentioned the story before now, or maybe he had, and she hadn't noticed any significant reason for it then.

She wished she could have met Miss Gwen in person. By the time they had moved into this house, she was around eight. Miss Gwen had died by then. She turned on her side suddenly feeling sleepy.

"Night Dad."

"Night Addi," he murmured closing his eyes too.

****

Addi went on to read book two of Gwendolyn Fisher's Diaries before she even ate breakfast. A point her mother wasn't reticent to share.

"I will eat," Addi mumbled in irritation. "I am fine."

Her mother paused before heading to the kitchen. "Breakfast is the most important meal of the day."

Addi looked over the top of the book. "Says who?"

"Says me." Her mother scowled. "And when since have you taken up back chatting me, Addison Porter? I hope this is not a thing."

Her full name. Her mother rarely used her full name unless she was about to get mad.

Addi sighed. She had to fly under the radar for two and a half more years. Acting like a teenager and not being to speak her mind was going to be a pain.

She could see it in her mother's nose flare. She could see it in the tapping of her feet.

Addi had better move now, or else she wouldn't hear the end of it. She had forgotten how grumpy her mother had gotten especially this summer.

The last time she had been happy to get out of the house then. She got up, feeling hard done by. Why should she be browbeaten to eat a meal she had no interest in? The 2000's had debunked the breakfast myth anyway.

Josh and Randy joined them just when her mother was about to blow her top. They had gone running.

"You could have invited me," Addi mumbled.

"You were snoring when we passed you on the settee," Randy was the first to quip. "There is always this evening."

Josh still had some residual resentment toward her for telling him bad things about his Ellie.

He just shrugged. "I wouldn't want you along with us anyway. You would slow us down."

Addi made a face at him and headed for the kitchen. Her mother had scrambled eggs and fried plantains and fried over dumplings. She didn't want it. She wished that her mother wasn't watching her so keenly waiting for a fight.

She sighed and took a generous amount just to avoid the eagle-eyed stare she was getting from that side of the kitchen.

It just struck her that this summer was not entirely trouble free for her parents as her earlier recollections had been. Her mother seemed worried about something. Maybe her ex-boyfriend who was coming to visit?

Addi would not dare ask her now.

Instead, she broke the silence by asking about the sewing machine.

"It's in there. I haven't used it in years." Her mother shrugged. "It was your grandmother's. She gave it to me when she migrated."

"Can I lend it to Myrna next door?" Addi asked.

"Who is Myrna?" Her mother asked puzzled.

By the time Addi finished explaining her mom was nodding vigorously. "Yes, that's a good idea. I even have some of my mom's supplies, in the music room somewhere."

"Thanks, Mom." Addi smiled happily.

Her mother nodded. "Imagine that. I had no idea that her name was Myrna. If she is good with the sewing thing, maybe I can be her first customer. I have to change some of these curtains in here."

"I already asked her to do some curtains for my room and a bedspread."

"And how are you going to pay for this?" Her mother raised her eyebrows.

"I am going to do some betting like Uncle Stan," Addi said quickly. "The US vice presidential pick is coming up."

Her mother opened her mouth to protest. Her father came

into the kitchen at the same time.

"Who are you betting on? There is Kerrey, Hamilton, Graham, Gore, Wofford..."

"Are you serious?" Her mother gasped. "Nate you can't encourage gambling!"

"When you ask me to buy a raffle ticket for the mothers union at church what is that?" Her dad snorted. "And your Lions club fundraising ticket for the car of my dreams and your horticultural toaster raffle?"

"It's for a good cause!" Her mother almost squealed. "A noble cause!"

"And so is Addi's thing. Don't tell me gambling is bad only when it's not a church or established charity?" Her father sneered.

Her mother shook her head. "I can't argue with you...I can't..."

She left the kitchen.

Addi pushed over her plate to her dad.

He grinned at her. "She's right you know you shouldn't be gambling."

"It's not a gamble if you know who it is," Addi said simply. "I know who he is going to choose."

"Really now, you are that sure?" Her father tucked into her eggs. "Had no idea you were into US politics."

Addi suppressed a laugh. She had a doctorate in Sociology, a master's in political science. She was the youngest tenured professor in her field at her university...well she would be if she took that route again.

Maybe she could use her knowledge of the future and make some money and make this second time around more about learning things she had always wanted to learn.

Or maybe this time around she could write a book or two or ten.

"So who is it?" Her father broke into her little reverie. "Who is the certain pick?"

"Al Gore." Addi grinned. "You betting?"

"No." Her father reached into his wallet and extracted four fifty-dollar bills and gave it to her." Five to one odds on Gore. I should get back a thousand by this evening if you are right. We can split it."

Addi grinned. "Thanks, Dad."

"If you are wrong." Her father winked, "we never talk about this again, at least not in front of your mother."

****

She was right, as she knew she would be. Randy solemnly gave her a stack of hundred and fifty dollars tied up in rubber bands. He carried it in his knapsack and laid them out beside her in the settee. She had just finished the juicy story of Miss Gwen's meeting with her husband, Captain Charles Donald Campbell. They got married when she was sixteen.

Addi dragged her eyes from the pages and looked at the piles and piles of money and felt like the Grandfather.

"How much is it?" She whispered as she saw the stacks of money that wouldn't quit.

"Fifty-one thousand," Randy said. "I gave them ten thousand. So that's five times ten and your dad's two hundred which is now a thousand."

"Wow," Addi put away the book and looked at the money feeling slightly dazed.

"Yes, wow." Randy didn't look at all happy. He sat down heavily beside the money.

"You wanted me to be wrong?" Addi asked him puzzled.

"Yes." Randy sighed. "Addison, this just confirms that your claims are not as off the wall and crazy as I had thought that they were in the first place."

"I thought I had cleared that up." Addi got up and stretched.

"Well, I had doubts." Randy shook his head. "When the announcement was made today on both TV and radio because the guys had to be sure, I had this urge to run out of the building and hide."

"Why?" Addi looked at him sharply.

"Because of my future..." he swallowed, "you know my future. I've been skirting the issue of my future with you. I have a feeling that I don't want to know. And yet, I do. Makes sense?"

"Yes." Addi nodded. "I went absurd on you the day I met you and then declaring that we were lovers. I can understand the reluctance."

"So why weren't we married?" Randy asked cautiously.

"You married someone else," Addi said simply.

Randy opened his mouth and then closed it. "I did? Who?"

"I am not going to tell you anything else about her," Addi said simply. "It would be wicked of me to try to influence your life like that."

"Well...did I love her?"

"I don't know. I didn't want to know." Addi sighed. "You stayed with her. That's enough."

"I had an affair." Randy shook his head. "Nah, sounds wrong. Doesn't sound like me."

"It doesn't have to be. You can be faithful to your wife, whosever she is." Addi started to count the money. "You won't be cheating with me. I know for myself, I am going to find a nice guy. It shouldn't be hard. There are a couple of candidates that I know of, both in Jamaica and the US, who are faithful to their wives and totally sweet. I'll just see who I can snatch before they meet their significant others."

Randy looked at her incredulously, and then he started to

laugh.

Addi ignored him. "I am going to get married by the time I am twenty-three or so, and then I am going to have at least three children. I want them early. Last time I got pregnant when I was..."

She stopped moving.

Randy too.

"Who was the father?" Randy finally asked.

"Only one candidate. No other man in my life. Ever." She shoved a stack of money back into his bag. "There it is fifty-fifty."

"We had a child together?" Randy asked weakly.

"No, we didn't. He died." Addi sniffed and then looked at him. "Losing a child is the worst pain ever."

Randy sighed. "How did I handle it?"

"You had a lot on your plate at that time," Addi sat back in the settee. "Your wife had a baby too."

Randy winced.

"And you had a junior pastor who wanted your post. He was getting the necessary backing of your church board to oust you because you were coming to the US so much, you wanted to be there for me. And your wife, she wanted you around too. You were pulled in a million and one directions, and I needed you the most. I think I almost went mad."

"I was a minister?" Randy shook his head, "that's how I know that this is fiction. Accounting is my first love. Construction engineering a close second. Working with your dad and uncle, I am unsure which one to pursue in the future. I am not going to be a minister.

"You were good at it." Addi shrugged, "Your people loved you."

"How did I manage a moral dilemma like the one you just described, though?" Randy shook his head. "And for twenty years? Why didn't I just leave my wife if I was that into you?"

Addi inhaled raggedly. "We tried to end it. We really did. Every year we had this final and complete severance speech, but we were to each other like opiates."

"Drugs?" Randy snorted.

"Yes, but we had a relapse every summer. Every single summer. It seems as if summers were our thing." Addi laughed mirthlessly. "Except for the first time."

"The first time?" Randy murmured.

"Yes, the first time we kissed. Made love. You found me at the university. I was living off campus in an apartment near the school. January 1996. I'll probably never forget it. Ever. And I shouldn't be telling you any of this."

"No, go on," Randy said huskily, "it's kind of fascinating."

"You got married two months before. I hated you for it. I begged you not to do it. So when you showed up at my door, I was not pleased with you. Not one bit. I fondly thought you'd wait for me, you know, like one of those epic love films where the guy and girl waited for each other despite the odds?"

Randy nodded.

"So anyway, you show up. You tell me you missed me; you complained that I wasn't answering any of your calls and then you told me that you couldn't do any of this without me. Then contrarily you ask me to send you away. You wanted me to tell you. I could have ended it then, but I didn't. I stepped into your arms like a homing pigeon, and we spent two weeks together mostly naked. You missed the conference you came to the university for. I missed a couple of my classes."

Randy ran his hand over his face. "Future Randy sounds like a person I wouldn't like."

Addi was silent, and then she smiled. "I loved Future Randy. Crazily. Totally. Deeply."

Randy looked at her contemplatively. "How did it end?"

"You thought enough was enough and you ended it. Future Randy was a thousand times better than Future Addi. You did what you had to do."

"Twenty years later," Randy said softly. "For what it's worth, Addison Porter, I am sorry."

"You haven't done anything to be sorry for." Addi handed him back his knapsack. "Here is your half. Maybe next week we can go and get supplies for Myrna while we stake out Ellie. Kill two birds with one stone."

Chapter Fourteen

They were all invited to Aunt Ivy's for Sunday dinner. Josh declined. He had a date with Ellie. Her mother insisted on taking something to contribute to the meal and had volunteered to make bread pudding. A dish that was Aunt Ivy's specialty.

Addi watched her for a while as she flitted around the kitchen driving herself crazy trying to perfect the dish and only then did it dawn on her that her mother had a low-key competition going with her sister-in-law that Addi had not appreciated before.

It made sense.

Ivy had the expertise in homemaking. Ivy was a master chef and decorator had taught scores of top chefs in the industry.

It was almost suicidal for her mother to compete with Ivy. Her mother had confessed to her several years in the future that she only knew how to cook the basics when she got married and had leaned heavily on her mother for culinary support.

But now here was Victoria Porter, regular home cook, going up against Ivy Porter, a culinary genius with a dish Ivy could probably bake in her sleep and have people swooning over.

Addi couldn't watch. She made one small attempt to get her mother to stop in her quest.

"Mom, Aunt Ivy usually has desserts, and she is the queen of bread pudding."

"What did you say?" Her mother spun around.

She was still dressed in her church clothes, she had removed her hat and had put on an apron over her pink lace dress.

"Aunt Ivy is better at bread puddings than you," Addi said refusing to back down. "You are out of your depth here, and it shows."

"Get out!" Her mother screeched pointing the spatula at her. "Out! Only come back when you have confidence in your old mother to get this right for once."

Addi grinned. "Okay, but the truth is..."

"The truth is..." Vicky snorted, "I have been privately practicing. Now, if you'll take your negativity far from this kitchen, I can get on with this in peace."

"I am gone," Addi called as she headed to the veranda.

Randy and her father were reading the newspaper. They had a small pile of it between them. She couldn't see their faces.

She sat across from them and pushed out her tongue in a juvenile gesture.

She picked up the Sunday magazine from the pile and skimmed through it. It was interesting to look in the Social Pages and on the fashion in 92. Shoulder pads were in.

Her father grunted and lowered his paper.

"Addi, what's going on?"

"Nothing," she looked up at him and smiled. "Just thought I would join you out here. Mom is in the kitchen going crazy trying to outdo Aunt Ivy with bread pudding."

Her father laughed and picked up the next piece of newspaper. "Your mom's bread pudding is better than anybody else's in the whole world."

"You are biased," Addi muttered.

"Hey ho," Uncle Stan walked on the veranda and sat down next to Addi, "I am supposed to tell you all that dinner will be at three-thirty promptly."

Her father grunted.

Addi looked at her uncle and nodded. "We heard."

Stan shrugged. "What's interesting in the news?"

"Jamaica getting ready for the Olympics." Randy lowered his section of the paper and handed it to Stan. "I know you will want to read this."

"Oh yes." Stan was on the verge of salivating. "Oh yes. I can't wait for the Olympics. I am putting all I have on Merlene Ottey to win the hundred and two hundred meters."

"Don't forget Juliet Cuthbert." Nate piped in. "She is looking good."

Stan shrugged. "I don't know. Ottey for me."

"Who are you betting on to win the track events?" Her father looked at her thoughtfully.

Randy was looking at her too, no expression on his face.

Addi looked at the men. "Why are you asking me?"

"Because you made us all a boatload of money last time." Her uncle said widening his eyes. "I had no idea it would have been Gore, but Randy here said you were a 100 percent certain, so I followed him. And bam, I made a hundred thousand just like that. Thanks, Addi."

Addi teased them. "Glad I could help. Hope you are putting

some of that money into Sky's college fund. My daddy said I shouldn't gamble."

"But you said you were sure," Her father muttered, "and you ended up being right. So, who do you like for the events?"

Addi closed her eyes and tried to remember results. In the time before she had watched the events with her uncle, Randy, and Josh.

At least now she knew why her uncle and father were so devastated over some of the results. They had been betting over the outcomes. She had been quite oblivious to that then.

The two of them were waiting with bated breath now as she wracked her brain.

"Okay," she finally said, "for the men 100 meters, the winner is Linford Christie from Great Britain, second is Frankie Fredericks from Namibia, and Dennis Mitchell from the United States, third.

Her uncle dragged out a pen out of his pocket and a small notebook and started jotting down information.

"Wait, are you sure?" Her father was looking doubtful. "How can you be so sure?"

"Because I am a time traveler," she said it seriously, "I've lived this life before. I know all of this. I especially know this because you had me writing down results for you before. I tend to remember things I write down."

Her uncle nodded. "That's a good reason. Time travel. If I could time travel, I would write down the lottery numbers for every big year. And Sweepstakes. Not to mention horses. And I would definitely invest in upcoming stocks.

"What about the women 100m?"

"Gail Devers from the US, first, Juliet Cuthbert from Jamaica, second and Irina Privalova, from The Unified Team, third."

"What on earth a unified team?" Her uncle asked her

puzzled.

"It was a joint team consisting of twelve of the fifteen former Soviet republics." Addi said, "They were the top medal finishers too."

"Wait!" her father held up his hand. "Stan, Addi does not know any of this for sure. So please, if you lose any money please do not blame my daughter!"

"I won't blame her." Uncle Stan was busy jotting down her information quite oblivious to her father's caution. "I will do my own calculations based on the semifinals, but this is a good start. Never hurts to hear other people's predictions especially because she is a time traveler."

Randy looked at her and smiled, shaking his head. "The Unified Team was in today's sporting section."

"Oh," her father who was more perturbed about her story than she had given him credit for relaxed and sighed. "For a minute there, I thought Addi was a real time traveler!"

Addi smirked. "I am dad."

He picked up another piece of paper. "No, you aren't. There is no such thing."

He got lost in another piece of newspaper effectively shutting her out.

Uncle Stan looked at her contemplatively. "You don't happen to know about horses do you?"

"No." Addi shook her head.

"Lottery numbers?"

"No," Addi said again.

"What about stocks?"

"Technology." Randy was the one who answered, "You would be half blind not to see that this is where the world is heading. Apple and Microsoft are two names to keep in mind."

He remembered that from their conversation. Addi opened

her mouth in awe and looked at him.

Randy winked.

She looked across at Uncle Stan who was jotting down the names.

"Uncle Stan, you seriously believe that I am a time traveler?" Addi asked incredulously.

"Yes." Her uncle winked at her, "why wouldn't I?"

She didn't know if she should take him seriously.

****

As usual Aunt Ivy had cooked up a scrumptious meal quite devoid of any imperfections.

She had the atmosphere just right. It was overcast, so she turned on the chandelier, which sat directly over the exquisitely set table. She obviously had a theme, white and gold. And in pure Ivy style, she was not doing anything in half measures. Everything was elaborate and looked like it belonged in a five-star restaurant.

Addi saw her mother shudder with jealousy when they entered the house. She couldn't resist a grin at her mother who pointedly ignored her. She had the still hot bread pudding in the tin with thick oven mitts holding it slightly away from her body.

"Oh, Victoria, you shouldn't have." Ivy looked shocked at the offering. "I already did crème brûlée for dessert. To be served with homemade ice cream."

"Okay then," her mother said brightly as if she hadn't been slaving away at the pudding. "I'll just take this back over then."

"I am so sorry, Victoria," Ivy said not looking one bit sorry. "We'll wait for you until you return."

She turned to them. "In the meantime, let us be seated and

wait for Victoria's return."

Addi watched the dynamics between the two women and marveled that she hadn't seen this underlying animosity before.

She ended up sitting beside Randy as usual. He was not oblivious to the undercurrents, and he raised his eyebrows at her. "This is my first time over here. It looks quite different from your house."

"Yep. Aunt Ivy is bourgeois." Addi nodded, "Wait until you taste the food."

"So where is Joshua?" Aunt Ivy asked pleasantly while they were all seated. "I was hoping that he would take his girlfriend with him to dinner. Like he did at your place last week. What is her name again?"

"Ellie," Addi said politely.

"Ellie." Aunt Ivy repeated the name. "Is it short for Eleanor or Ellen, do you know?"

"No." Addi shook her head. "I thought it was just Ellie. I thought you would know better than me since she goes to your school."

"That she does." Ivy smiled coldly. "Well then..." She looked at the table at large. "Our family seems to be dwindling without us even realizing. Skyler is at Colleen's, and Joshua is out with this Ellie.

"What is her surname again Addison?"

Addi started to feel uncomfortable. She felt as if she was under some kind of inquisition. She wished her aunt would stop questioning her in that stiff fraught manner.

Her father and uncle were quiet. Both of them sipping water and not saying anything to break up the attention or to keep the conversation going.

"Her name is Ellie Dunn," Addi said quickly. Feeling relieved when her mother entered the dining room without the pudding or anything in her hand for that matter.

"Have a seat, Victoria," Ivy said gesturing to the chair closest to her. "We were talking about Joshua and his new girlfriend, Ellie."

"Oh," Vicky smiled. "She's a lovely girl. Very nice."

"I would think so. Porter men have great taste in women." Ivy looked at her husband and brother-in-law a hint of frost in her eyes.

Her dad and uncle smiled politely. Neither of them said a word.

"And we were discussing that her surname was Dunn." Ivy continued, "Do you know that her uncle Jerome Dunn owns Mack J's?"

"I didn't know his name, but she said her uncle owned it," Vicky said smiling.

Ivy got up and lifted up the covers to the shiny platters off the dishes. "You should visit there sometime Victoria, quite an interesting place especially on Monday's."

"Mondays," Vicky widened her eyes, "why Mondays?"

"They come up with some surprising dishes after the weekend," Ivy said, "Well that's enough chatter about it, let's eat."

Chapter Fifteen

Mack J's was a medium sized restaurant located at the corner of a plaza. The plate glass window had a huge sign on the front, followed by the words breakfast, lunch, and diner. Obviously a typo with one 'n' missing.

The interior was large enough that they could check out Ellie and not be spotted immediately. There were a few palm plants strategically placed around the room to make the place look better and to give diners a sense of privacy.

Addi was grateful for that because she was sure that when she and Randy arrived a little past lunch time that Ellie would recognize them immediately even though she had dressed like a boy in baggy shirt and pants that were a size too big, she had a baseball cap firmly lodged on her head. It was pulled down almost completely covering her eyes.

Randy was in jeans and a dress shirt and baseball cap too.

They sat in the back of the restaurant in the seats furthest from the door. They could clearly see Ellie, but she had yet to look in their direction or pay them any attention.

So far so good. Addi thought, feeling tenser than she should.

That morning they had started a little later than she had hoped. Her father and uncle Stan had lingered longer than she expected. They had finally gone on their way at least after eleven in the morning, and then there was the rain. As it was in the time before, the rain had started in earnest. It would last the week.

"Why did you think your aunt was so insistent on your mom coming here?" Randy asked looking at the menu. "There is nothing on the menu that is unusual, curry chicken, stewed chicken, baked chicken. It's all chicken."

"I know." Addi nodded. "She was acting weird yesterday. And in the timeline before this, we never had a Sunday dinner."

Randy nodded. "It was a bit cold and stuffy over there, but the food was good. It's the first time that I had crème brûlée."

"She does it all the time." Addi shrugged. "It is supposed to be hard to do or something. I had a piece of my mom's bread pudding after and I have to say that it was better."

Randy chuckled.

"Can't remember it tasting that good." Addi shook her head. "My mom must have been practicing."

"What does she do in the future?" Randy asked as they settled in, watching Ellie as she attended to several customers.

"She who?" Addi pulled her cap lower over her eyes.

"Your aunt Ivy," Randy said, following her gesture and doing the same.

"We migrated in 95, after the fire."

"Fire?" Randy raised an eyebrow.

"Yes, the warehouse, where the hardware store is, burnt to the ground. My grandma was filing for us before that.

My dad had not wanted to go but Uncle Stan wasn't around anymore, the business was up in flames. I had just finished high school, and I got a very high SAT score, and my mom was depressed.

"We packed up and left. Aunt Ivy was still living at the house. Sky got a scholarship and went to Harvard Business. Her grades in the SAT were exceptionally good."

"Wow, you serious? Your cousin, is a Harvard graduate?"

"Yep." Addi nodded, "she has a scary knack for figures and what will make things work.

"Sky was the one who sent for Aunt Ivy. Aunt Ivy lived with Sky in New York for several years. She worked for a catering firm for a while. Sky made some investments for her, and she was living quite comfortably.

"We never really saw her much, unless Sky dragged her to a family gathering. If it weren't for Sky, we wouldn't have seen her at all over the years."

"So what did you do in the future?" Randy asked lazily.

They watched Ellie at the cash register for a while. She was very popular with the customers, that much was obvious. Many of them greeted her by name.

There was one particular guy, who the girls at the counter greeted as Ray when he walked into the restaurant. He was a construction worker, he had on a yellow hard hat and had a pencil behind his ear, and he was shamelessly flirting with Ellie as well as with the other girls who were serving.

"That may be him," Addi whispered.

"Why?" Randy asked puzzled.

"Because she is flirting back," Addi said taking out her little notebook which she had carried just for this very purpose and wrote down the name Ray. "She doesn't flirt back with anyone."

Randy chuckled. "But we've only been here for what, thirty

minutes? Maybe she flirts with a guy every thirty minutes."

"Maybe," Addi murmured. "But this guy is going on my list. He looks suspicious."

"You didn't answer my question." Randy leaned closer to her. "What do you do in the future?"

"I had a bachelor in sociology, went on to do my master's in political science and then doctorate in the same sociology. I chose different emphasis each time. I did a brief stint in advertising after the first degree. Then I worked as a Research Director after the masters, and then after the doctorate, I worked as a professor at a university."

"So you are a doctor?" Randy opened his eyes wide, "like an honest to goodness Ph.D.?"

Addi nodded. "Yes. But now I have to redo high school. How is that for irony?"

"High school should be a breeze for you." Randy chuckled. "Imagine all the scholarships you can get. You could get to go anywhere! Harvard! Oxford! Anywhere!"

He pulled his cap lower on his head and sunk down in the seat as Ray came closer to them with his tray of food.

Addi followed him making sure her face was not visible behind the plant.

Ray sat at the table closest to them and started eating his food.

They watched him as he watched Ellie.

He had it bad. It was obvious that he had an enormous crush on her. Addi felt like crowing, I told you so!

When Ellie left the cash register and came over to their end of the restaurant, Addi almost gasped aloud. This was too easy. She had anticipated stalking her for at least a week and maybe some guesswork. But here she was gliding toward Ray with a small smile on her face.

She sat down beside him, her side view visible to Addi.

"Hey," Ellie was speaking low, but Addi could hear, so could Randy.

He gave Addi a shocked look.

"Where is my thing?"

"Here it is," Ray took out a broad white envelope and set it down before her.

"How are you doing?"

"Fine." Ellie took the letter folded it in two and tucked it in her jeans pocket.

"You know I can take care of you." Ray reached over the table and touched her hand. Ellie pulled it away.

"No thanks, Ray. I am fine."

"He doesn't deserve you," Ray grunted. "You could do better. He's married. I am not. What do you find so attractive about him? The Monday morning money? I can do that. Not because he's the boss, I can get my own jobs; I can do anything he does."

Addi looked at Randy sharply. She was right! But not about Ray!

A married man? Was Ellie seeing a married man? Somebody who gave her money on a regular basis. Ray's boss? No wonder she hadn't wanted anyone to know who the father of her baby was.

"You should ditch him, be with me," Ray offered grinning. "I can be good to you."

"No thanks." Ellie got up. "Not interested. And who says we are involved?"

She got up and pushed in her chair.

Ray shrugged. "I am just the messenger telling it like how I see it. By the way, compliments to the chef. Tell your uncle that he is the best damned cook in the entire Jamaica, if not the entire world!"

Ellie smiled. "I'll tell him."

Randy waited until she was a distance away before he got up. "Let's go, Addi."

"But why?" Addi pointed to Ray. "He is still eating."

"Come on," Randy was almost through the door before Addi reacted.

"What was that about?" Addi ran into the car and swiped the cap from her head. "Start talking."

Randy turned his head to look at her and then sighed. "I know who Ray is."

"So tell me." Addi could barely contain her excitement. "Does that mean you have an idea who Ellie's married man is?"

Randy looked at her sadly, "Maybe, maybe not."

"Who is he?" Addi pinched him, "just say it. Don't leave me in suspense."

"I think it would be better if we confirm it before I jump to conclusions." Randy nodded seeming as if he had come to a decision. "We should follow him to work."

Addi settled down in her seat. Watching the restaurant door intently. Her curiosity was now more than stoked especially as Randy had gone mysterious on her.

So Ellie was a two-timing slut who was sleeping with a married man along with her brother or would be sleeping with her brother.

"You can't judge her." Randy piped into her thoughts as if he were a mind reader. "Weren't you with a married man for twenty years?"

"You were the married man, and you are right, I shouldn't judge her. But please note, you and I won't happen again," Addi hissed. "And because it won't happen. I was never an adulteress. I am so sorry I told you."

"Nope, you were quite happy to tell me." Randy chuckled. "You couldn't wait to blurt it out the minute you saw me. I thought you were Josh's mad little sister with a hell of an imagination. But you aren't...no one could make up this kind of thing."

He said it grimly.

Randy started the car when Ray walked out of the restaurant.

Ray got into a battered green truck and drove out of the parking lot.

Randy followed him at a steady pace as he drove out of town toward Ingleside.

Addi always loved coming to Ingleside. It had a lot of gorgeous houses and superb views of the surrounding hills. It was also the place where her father and uncle were building an apartment complex.

Ray turned into a marled driveway, into what was obviously a construction site and stopped.

Randy turned in with him.

"What are you doing?" Addi hissed. "He is going to see us."

"I know," Randy said grimly. "He is supposed to see me. I am supposed to check up with him every day. You know he is the foreman in charge while your father and uncle are away."

Addi gasped. "What? No!"

"Yes." Randy nodded. "Your father said that I should speak with Ray. His full name is Raymond Byfield. I should know, I did the payroll roll last week, and this is the site."

Addi was shaking her head, and she didn't even know she was doing it. "No way."

"Yes," Randy nodded. "I guess you can narrow Ellie's list of married men to two men. Your father or your uncle. They are Ray's bosses."

Addi could not wrap her mind around it. She couldn't. It

wasn't shocking. That was too mild a word. It was mind-boggling.

She was confused. One didn't want to think of her beloved father or uncle cheating.

****

Her mattress came later in the evening, and she watched the deliverymen and Josh as they put it on her bed frame.

She felt as if she was watching from a far distance like this was not happening. The news had finally sunk in. One of her dear loved ones had cheated on his wife, her mother or aunt, with Ellie, her brother's girlfriend.

One of them, either her father or her uncle, had conspired to get Josh take responsibility for their child.

She had spent most of the afternoon shopping for sheets and material for her bedspread and curtains. She did not want to think about it. Randy had been her silent shadow, not seeming as if he wanted to speak about it either.

Now the knowledge of what she learned today, suddenly and brutally grabbed her and wouldn't let go. She spread the bed with her new sheets and then laid on it looking up into the ceiling.

The bed felt good.

Perfect. Not a squeak as she turned in it. No more sleeping in settees for her.

She had to sort through this conundrum though. All that she had thought that she knew about her time this summer had been a lie. She didn't know squat, but it seemed as if her aunt Ivy knew something. All of that barely controlled hostility yesterday and those broad hints about visiting Mack J's and bringing up Ellie's name doggedly was a message to one of the men.

But which one?

Both of them had gone silent when Ivy had started on her Ellie questions.

A two-tap knock on her door had her rolling over and closing her eyes she didn't want to talk to anyone. Not now.

"Come in," she mumbled closing her eyes.

"Mom said you wanted to move a sewing machine next door."

Addi cracked her eyes open. Josh had been treating her cold lately, and it was spilling over into his voice now.

"I'll have to clean out the music room," she said closing her eyes again. "Maybe tomorrow."

Josh nodded, but she could still hear him standing there.

"What you said about Ellie was hurtful," he said stiffly. "I mean I like your guess the future games, I really do, but Addi, this is Ellie we are talking about. She is my girlfriend. We are getting serious."

Addi grunted. "It's not a future game."

"Well, whatever you want to call it. Don't say anything about Ellie, okay."

"Fine," Addi said feeling drained of energy. She felt like shrieking at him, but this was not his fault. He was a patsy for either his father or uncle and she had a sneaky feeling that Ellie had singled him out in the past couple of weeks for just this reason.

She took one of her pillows and covered her head.

Josh left the room, and she heard the door click shut.

She removed the pillow and went back to staring at the ceiling. Stanley Carlos Porter and Nathan Robert Porter.

The Porter Brothers.

Stanley was barely a year older than Nathan. They were both close. They built their houses in the same yard. They ran the same business. They both married their college sweethearts.

Stanley married Ivy Richards in June 1974, and Nathan married Victoria Wallace in June 1975.

They had children at almost the same time too. Ivy had a son, Leroy in October 1975 who died from sudden infant death syndrome in 1976 and Victoria had Joshua Oneil the same year, who was still alive.

They both had daughters in 1977. Ivy had Skyler Simone in January 1980, and Victoria had Addison Monique February 1980.

The wives lived beside each other, but they managed to keep out of each other's space. Her mother had once told her that Ivy had never forgiven her for having a son who was still healthy and alive when hers died.

They had old baggage. Even in the future, Aunt Ivy pretty much kept to herself, only attending family get-togethers if Sky insisted.

One of these two women had a cheating husband. Addi breathed in tremulously. She hoped it wasn't her father.

She crossed her fingers in a childish gesture of hope as if that would change anything. But if it wasn't her father it would be her uncle.

Her uncle who had met an untimely death in a couple weeks' time. His death had caused a void in her father's life that had been painful to watch.

She flipped on her belly and tried to piece together any clues from the past that would point to Ellie being attached to any of them. She was drawing blanks.

But wait, her mind started to tick feverishly.

Before, when Josh had found out that the child wasn't his, her father had readily offered to bail him out.

When Josh had insisted on marriage, her father had not convinced him otherwise. He hadn't been strident about it.

When Josh announced that Ellie was pregnant, her father had not acted all that surprised. He had just stiffened in shock. Her mother was the one who had gone into histrionics.

Maybe because she had known the truth and was sorrowful that her son was the one who was going to be sacrificed?

No, that theory was ridiculous. He mother was not going to allow her son to take the blame for anyone's indiscretion. Or would she?

Addi couldn't lie down with all the information running through her head. She had to run it by Randy. She flung open her door. And was about to head to the office when she saw Randy sitting in the settee with a newspaper in hand.

"You look like hell." He greeted her calmly.

"I think she knew," Addi said ignoring his comment on her disheveled appearance. "I think my mom knew about Ellie."

"Keep your voice down," Randy said lowering the paper. "Why would you say that?"

"Because..." Addi walked closer. "Before, when Josh announced that he found the woman he was going to marry and said it was Ellie, my dad was not very surprised. He just told Josh to finish school. He was the one who probably told Ellie to go out with his own son."

Randy raised an eyebrow. "No. Just no."

"Yes." Addi nodded. "I think my mom knew about Ellie and was happy that her husband's mistress had moved on, so she encouraged it."

Randy folded the paper and was staring at her his hands folded on his chest a look of incredulity on his face.

"And then when she got pregnant my mom was devastated because she knew who the father was."

"I don't think so." Randy shook his head.

"They offered to take care of Nelson when he was born. They paid Josh's rent while he was married to Ellie and still sent him to finish university; they bent over backward to help Ellie while she was pregnant. All without complaining. And one day I found my dad crying over Josh not getting his scholarship!"

"That just makes them parents." Randy sighed, "good ones. Not part of an insane conspiracy to trap Josh."

"No, I am right." Addi stopped pacing. "You know, I couldn't understand why they didn't know that Ellie was sleeping here at nights."

Randy watched her in fascination as she paced from one end of the living room to the other.

"I think you shouldn't jump to conclusions, Miss Sherlock."

"Everything is so obvious to me now," Addi whispered her voice hoarse.

"I hope it doesn't have anything to do with me, whatever it is," Sky said behind her. Addi spun around her cousin was standing there with a sheepish look on her face.

"I am back. Couldn't stay away from you for long. What's going on?"

Chapter Sixteen

"**I** hate when you give me the silent treatment," Sky said following her to her room.

Addi didn't answer. She headed straight for the bookcase where she was storing Sky's book and handed it to her.

"What happened in here?" Sky looked around.

"I am redecorating," Addi smirked. "If you were around you would have seen me doing it, and you could have helped."

"Sorry. Nice color. In here looks bigger." Sky finally registered that she was holding the book and looked down at it. For Sky Porter's Eyes Only.

"What's this?"

"That is yours. You gave it to me in your will," Addi said sitting down on the bed and looking at Sky.

Sky clutched the book to her and grimaced at the word 'will'. She sat down. "I kissed Rusty."

Addi groaned. "Really?"

"Yep." Sky nodded. "The earth didn't shatter, and flowers didn't explode into bloom."

Addi chuckled. "Tragic."

Sky shrugged. "He lives near to Colleen, you know? That's why I went to stay with her so that I could see him. I hardly saw him though, and then a couple of nights ago I was going to the shop for Colleen, and he walked me home, and after that, he kissed me. I don't think the whole kissing thing is as interesting as the movies portray it to be."

"It depends on who you kiss." Addi wrinkled her brow. "Now, are you ready to focus on the time traveling thing I told you about?"

Sky nodded. "Yes, I guess. It's crazy though."

Addi pulled out her pouch where she had stored some of her winnings from the betting pool and opened it.

"This is what I got from betting correctly on Bill Clinton's vice president pick."

Sky's eyes opened wide. "What the hell?"

"Yup. While you were away pursuing a romance with Rusty, I was trying to get things done. You sent me back here to reset things! I don't care if you don't know that you did it, you are going to have to sober up and help me. It's time!"

"Okay!" Sky winced, "you don't have to shout. I am here aren't I?"

"Good." Addi snorted. "I hope that you wrote something down in that book that can help us to figure out how to save Uncle Stan from being killed."

Sky's eyes widened. "Who killed my dad?"

"Rusty." Addi didn't temper the news. "He pushed Uncle Stan off the second floor of the Ingleside job site."

She watched as Sky seemed to quail when she heard the news, she slumped down on the bed and curled up into a fetal position.

"And we need to figure out which one of our father's is seeing Josh's girlfriend." Addi spat out, "because pretty soon one of them is going to impregnate her and then Josh is going to be left carrying the bag."

Sky whimpered.

"And we need to know what kind of secret you had this summer that was so bad that you sent me back to fix."

Sky looked up at that. "I don't have any secrets!"

"Not yet," Addi growled, she was showing Sky no mercy. "But you will have one. In the meantime, stay away from murderous Rusty! I hope sleeping with him wasn't your secret."

"No way!" Sky exclaimed seeming to come back to life. "Well, it can't be, not now, not if he killed my dad."

"Good. Keep it that way," Addi muttered. She was feeling militant, irritable and unaccountably angry. She shouldn't be taking it out on Sky. She wanted to take it out on either her uncle or her dad.

Silence reigned in the room while Sky digested all of the news, she had just thrown at her.

"Tell me about Josh's girlfriend," Sky said quietly.

"He recently started seeing her," Addi said, by the time she finished telling Sky about the previous timeline and what happened now.

Sky was shaking her head. "That's sick!"

"I know." Addi sighed.

"Maybe it's my dad," Sky said after a prolonged silence.

"Really?" Addi sat up and looked at her cousin. "Why?"

"Because he and my mom are arguing a lot lately. It's crazy. They think I don't hear, but I do. They are both unhappy with each other. It was another reason why I went to Colleen's. My house is like a freezer. They don't talk anymore. It's like living with two robots that are pretending to like each other in front of me. I wouldn't be surprised if Dad is seeing someone else."

"That would explain the frigid atmosphere yesterday at Sunday dinner," Addi said thoughtfully. "Something seemed off."

Sky groaned. "I could have told you all of this the other day, but I had exams, and then there was your announcement that you were forty and you are from the future."

"Focus, Sky. The sooner we solve this conundrum, the better. It would make sense if it were Uncle Stan; Ellie had looked a little bit too drawn and sickly in October. She could have been grieving at the same time instead of being sick as we had originally thought."

Sky shuddered. "I need to meet this Ellie girl. Why don't we just accost her? Blurt out what we know. Point fingers. Crush her."

"No." Addi shook her head vehemently. "None of that. We are dealing with people here. Feelings and relationships. Gosh, my brother is so in love with her it's sickening.

"And if one of our fathers is the culprit then it would be a disaster for the family on a whole. Somebody's mother is going to be hurt. Josh is going to be hurt."

Sky sighed and then inspected the book. "I am feeling a bit scared to open this."

Addi shrugged. "You are the one who wrote it."

"And that is what makes it so strange," Sky muttered getting up. "But I'll read it. I'll tell you if there is anything interesting in it."

Addi nodded and then felt an overwhelming need to hug Sky. She looked so forlorn and burdened as if her young shoulders carried the weight of the world.

"Hey come here."

Sky looked at her wearily. "What?"

"I am happy you came back home now and that you are taking this seriously."

She hugged Sky and then stood back. "You know in the future I am taller than you."

"Rubbish." Sky sat down on the bed and then tried to open the taped edges of the notebook.

Addi watched her hardly daring to breathe. She wondered what Sky had written to herself. Would she finally know what the big secret was this summer?

"I need scissors or something sharp to cut around this," she looked at the book in irritation. "Why did I have to tape it so thoroughly?"

Addi got up and handed her a small paper scissors from her writing desk.

Sky slowly and methodically cut around the edges of the book and then opened it.

Addi breathed a sigh of relief. "Finally!"

"But there is nothing in here," Sky skipped through the book from the front to the back.

Addi looked at the thing. It was blank. What a letdown!

"Why would you send yourself a blank book?" Addi sat down beside Sky and looked at the thing in consternation. "You made this whole production of leaving me a letter and telling me where to spread your ashes and then...this, nothing?"

Sky sighed and leaned back on the bed. "Something must have gone wrong when you time traveled with it."

"Yes," Addi muttered feeling peeved. She thought that this would have been the big reveal. She had been counting on that book to tell them what to do next.

"What would future me, have to say?" Sky asked looking at Addi.

"Lots," Addi muttered. "Knowing you, you would probably

have stocks and share prices and when to buy and sell currencies. And maybe which guy not to date. And maybe who you are supposed to align yourself to for friendships and who to avoid in the business arena. Which deals are more profitable et cetera... et cetera."

"And how to wear my hair and which parties to attend and which fashion trends are going to be hot," Sky said salivating. "And sketches of clothes before they become a thing."

Addi laughed. "You are such a teenager. I keep forgetting that you are only fifteen and that you were... are fashion mad."

Sky sniffed. "I am a mature fifteen. And I am not fashion mad. I am going to be a designer."

"Nope." Addi shook her head. "You are good at business. You thrived in the cutthroat world. It is your domain. Men and women quake when you walk down the corridors of the glass partitions toward your office. You dress in nothing, but Gucci and other brand names and you are lethal."

"And yet I killed myself." Sky sighed, "Somewhere along me thriving I was dying inside. Maybe you didn't know me quite as well as you think, Addi."

Addi looked at her sharply. It was an astute observation and very accurate. "You wrote me a letter saying that something happened this summer that was so secretive you couldn't tell me."

Sky nodded. "Maybe I should just lock up in my room and not come out this summer then. That would be a solution."

"Or it would just let whatever happened before happen again." Addi felt little tremors of disappointment as she spoke. It was going to be up to her to navigate through this summer with her foreknowledge.

The ball was squarely back in her court. She didn't like this one bit.

Chapter Seventeen

Addi spent most of the next morning and part of the evening in the music room cleaning out boxes of hardware junk, debris from their lives, and old broken things from years gone by that her father had placed in the room because he was going to fix them. She even found a tricycle she had when she was five.

The work was slow going. The room was jam-packed with things. The sewing machine was buried under the various odds and ends.

It had seemed like a job for more than one person, but she had a system that was going pretty well.

She could hear the muted sounds of the Zorro television series Randy was watching and then she heard talking and laughing when Josh came home. He was home earlier than usual—Ellie must have had something else to do this evening.

And then Sky's voice joined the conversation.

She didn't mind the solitude so far.

Sky had gone to the dentist with her mother. Randy had some errand to run for her father and uncle, and her mother had gone off to work earlier than usual to accept some new supplies.

She had carried over her radio and had a blast listening to the radio programs. Hearing the concerns of the day on the radio hotline shows, thinking that the more things changed, the more they stayed the same.

People were complaining about the same things in 92 that they complained about in 2017, a quarter of a century later the issues were the same.

She listened to them, and it prevented her from thinking too much. Even though for one second at around lunchtime, when it was time for the midday prayer on RJR, she had closed her eyes and felt overwhelmed.

The question had throbbed in her head: Was she the only resetter to have gone back in time?

How did the others handle it?

Had they even managed to change anything significantly or were they destined to live out their lives again with the same outcomes?

She had gone into introspection and had almost been bogged down with burdensome worry and then she had spotted a box filled with threads and needles and a gazillion odds and ends related to sewing.

She had gotten back down to the business of sorting through the music room.

"There is a piano in here!" Josh's voice broke into her reverie.

She spun around and looked at him. "Yup. That's why we call it the music room."

"I never realized that it was so big." Josh continued into

the room and sat on the piano bench. "My word, it even has windows!" He stepped over boxes and bags and walked toward the window. "I can't believe it."

Addi rolled her eyes. "You want to help me take out some of these hardware supplies to the garage? I would be so grateful."

Josh looked at the boxes she was pointing at. "Hardware supplies?"

"Yep. A lot of them. Pipe fittings and electrical stuff. And curtain rods. And other stuff I can't identify."

"Wow." Josh looked at her appreciatively. "You have become industrious. What's that?"

"Game Boys," Addi said glancing at the box he was pointing at. A whole lot of them. I don't know if they were meant for sale or what. I haven't seen one of these in ages."

Josh whooped with joy. "I am taking two. Randy and I can have some mad fun playing."

Addi shrugged, "I remember that the last time when we cleared all of this stuff out, Daddy was declaring how we could have sold them at the store. He even said he found stuff that could be used on the site, so I am just moving up the timeline a bit."

Josh didn't respond. He was busy salivating over his newly found Game Boy.

"Just put the hardware stuff in the garage and the construction stuff in the office," Addi said pointing to the boxes. "I already labeled them."

Josh nodded and did what he was told. Randy joined him, and they silently hefted box after box and cleared up quite a bit of space in the music room. Two single seater settees were revealed and bags and bags of old newspaper, some of them dating back to the early eighties.

Addi was tempted to keep them and read them but resisted

the urge they took up too much space, and it was dusty.

She hauled them through the kitchen, and that was where she saw Sky sprawled out in the settee reading Gwen Fisher's diaries.

"Hello to you too." She growled. She knew Sky had heard her working in the music room and had deliberately not come to help.

"Hi," Sky looked over the book. "I have something to read to you."

"Not now," Addi mumbled, "I am busy. Besides, I read the first two already."

"They were in order?" Sky laughed, "I guess this is Book 4? She entitles it: Resetters And Their Special Gift."

Addi stopped and looked around. "Yes?"

"Go with your garbage, when you are done moving around, I can come and read it to you."

Addi grunted and headed outside. When she returned, Sky was in the music room, sitting on the piano bench.

"In here is great! And big! We can turn it into a CXC study room next school year."

Addi groaned, "I forgot about that."

"Why would you care?" Sky asked, "you lived it already. It should be a breeze for you."

"Yes, I did the subjects, but I have not looked at the material in years," Addi muttered. "This is going to be tedious."

"Whatever." Sky chuckled. "Tell me what happened to Julia, Annette, and Tariq?"

"Julia and Annette?" Addi looked at her blankly. "Oh, that Julia and Annette? Our friends from high school."

"You are going to be overbearing." Sky rolled her eyes. "Yes, them, our friends. Our current friends. You and Julia are so tight sometimes I get jealous."

"We lost touch in 95 when I left Jamaica." Addi panted a

little, "Because of something in the future we called social media we got back in touch in 2010. She lost the weight. She owned a gym and became health conscious. We envy her body. For a good long year that's all we talked about, how good Julia looks."

"Now and then, we say hi to her on social media, but we grew apart, we have different interests. What happened to her this summer, again?"

"Went to the UK for holidays," Sky muttered, "and Annette went to the US."

"What happened to Annette?" Sky asked eagerly.

"Annette got married to a popular entertainer—had four kids for him. They are still together. They have a reality television show. She is a celebrity of sorts. Her oldest girl is an international model. Whenever I see her on television, I feel old."

Sky whistled. "Good for her. And Tariq?"

"Gay," Addi said hauling a bag through the door, "and out and very proud of it. In the future, you guys go shopping together."

Sky gasped. "What? No, Tariq isn't gay!"

"Yep." Addi stuck her head around the door. "You are supposed to find out five years from now when he tried to have a thing with you, and it didn't work out. You can thank me for the heads up now."

"Addi!" Sky called, walking behind her. "Tell me more about this."

"I don't know anything much, you must have tried to have sex with him or something, and it wasn't happening." Addi headed to the kitchen where Randy and Josh were drinking water thirstily.

Josh heard the last part of her statement and choked mid-gulp.

Addi rolled her eyes and headed for the back door. She dumped the next bag of newspapers in the incinerator. Three more and she could set it alight.

She was blocked at the door by a scowling Josh. "What's wrong with you?"

"Nothing." Addi matched his scowl with one of her own. "What's wrong with you?"

"You are going to stop this future nonsense stuff." Josh pointed at her, "or else I am going to tell Mom and Dad."

Addi glared at him. "Well, tell them. Please. Stage a family intervention for me."

Josh looked at her aghast as she called his bluff.

"Whatever you do will not prevent the fact that I am what I am. And I say the things that I know to be true of the future. I can't believe that you threatening to tell Dad and Mom on me worked in the past."

She brushed past him and looked back. "If you would just for one moment believe that I know the future it would save you a ton load of hurt!"

She walked toward the music room with Sky hurrying behind her.

She finished the music room in a huff. Sky finally chipped in to help her haul away the newspapers. And then her mother came home saw the machine sitting in the corner and the sewing supplies and started to get nostalgic about sewing.

"No," Addi shook her head. "I already promised to lend it to Myrna."

"Okay, okay," her mother looked around. "Good job, Addi."

"I am thinking of repainting in here and putting up a curtain at the window and turning this into a proper study," Addi said, "I have yet to put up the books on the shelves. Maybe I should move my desk in here."

Her mother nodded. "Sure, go ahead."

****

Addi and Sky accompanied Josh and Randy as they moved the sewing machine and other things next door. When Myrna saw them coming, she widened her eyes in astonishment. They set up in a large empty front room, with Myrna leaning on the door, tears in her eyes.

"Thank you, all of you, for the help. And Addison… I don't have the words."

"You are welcome," Addi said tiredly, being on her feet all day was catching up with her. "I'll take my material by tomorrow."

The four of them walked back over to the house mostly in silence. The air had a nippy bite to it even though the evening sun was still out and shining in its golden splendor.

Addi felt dusty and tired. Her little tiff with Josh had drained her somewhat. She didn't like when they had disagreements, and she especially hated the way that he was so strident against her talk of the future.

She went straight to her room with Sky walking behind her. "I didn't read the book about resetters to you."

"Can I bathe first?" Addi asked, "I feel filthy."

"Sure." Sky made herself comfortable on the bed and started skipping through the pages.

Addi was surprised to see that she was still engrossed in the book when she came out of the shower.

She pulled on a gray dress with bell sleeves and looked at herself in the mirror. It wasn't until next year that her breasts got bigger. She undid her bun and combed through her hair slowly.

"Are you going to try a bang?" Sky asked glancing at her.

"Nope." Addi shook her head. "Already did. Didn't like it."

Sky frowned. "Lucky you. You have already done your experimenting. Anyway, want to hear this?"

"Yes." Addi plaited her hair in two and left them hanging at the sides of her head. She looked like a young girl.

Too young. She was tempted to unravel them but resisted the urge.

"Are you listening, Miss Vanity?" Sky muttered.

"Yes, I am." Addi turned her attention to Sky.

"It says here, that resetters who have never traveled always have two distinct lines in their palms."

"Like I did before." Addi nodded. "Since I traveled my palms are full of lines like yours."

"Gwen Fisher says that one in every million babies born to this world are resetters. They can be found in every race, everywhere in this world. There are several pathways, on the planet, so far only four are rumored to be in Jamaica."

Addi nodded. "The blue stone on this land is one."

"The other three are not known for sure. There was this guy, Oswald King, from the 19th century who had an article about it in the Gleaner. She has a clip of it here." Sky pointed to the page.

"Gwen Fisher said that is where she got all of her information on resetters. She spotted the article in the archives while working at the library one day.

"Oswald King had a clue for all of the pathways. Like a treasure hunt kind of thing. Hear this. 'In a land that is cool, the stone is blue, palm to palm you'll know what to do."

"That's here." Addi grinned, "A land that is cool is Mandeville, and the stone here is blue."

"Do you know this one?" Sky read it slowly, "At the side of the road in plain sight covered in stone lays a resetter and his ride."

"Nah," Addi shook her head.

"How about this?" Sky was enjoying herself. "Nestled in a rock with grime and filth lays a gem in the midst of it, for a resetter do with it what he wilt."

Addi grinned. "Okay then. Vague."

"And this," Sky chuckled. "The keystone in the arch looks unassuming, but many a resetter has placed their hand on it and escaped a dooming."

"Ha." Addi shook her head. "Maybe I should solve the riddles and write a book about it."

Sky shrugged, "Good luck to you and that. Oswald King says that resetters can go back anywhere in their lives even their birth. He says that they can take back some things with them including rings, watches, photographs, and notebooks. But only if it was produced or available in the time in which they went back and clutched in their palms. Books with ink manufactured at a later time will only be blank books."

Addi widened her eyes. "That's why your book was blank!"

Sky nodded. "Maybe I used a fancy 21st-century pen to write notes to myself."

Addi shook her head. "Only you!"

"Well, I didn't know about this rule, obviously." Sky scowled. "Anyway, this guy says that resetters have been dabbling in time travel for centuries. Some were burnt at the stakes as witches and have been persecuted through the ages. They tend to keep a low profile, many of them choosing not to travel back in time because it was more trouble than it was worth.

"Oswald King says that in his first lifetime he met resetters who had tried to mess with the timeline of political events but never succeeded. He says that he has met resetters who tried to avert significant disasters but ended up creating another.

"He ends by saying that resetters should be mostly

observers. And that if you can avoid the past do so. Too late for you." Sky sniggered.

Addi lay down on the bed. "Yup, note to self: Never follow Sky Porter in anything again. That's all."

"Oh, and one more thing." Sky pointed at the article, "Resetters lose the memory of their previous life after a while. Some of them lose it all together; some retain snippets of it but only vaguely. If you go back, you have to act fast to change whatever it is you want to change because the longer you stay, the more likely you are to revert to who you were then."

Addi sighed. "So, I'll forget?"

Sky nodded. "Yep. You should write down stuff. Stuff that you don't want to repeat."

"Good idea." Addi nodded. "I will."

Sky closed the book. "Or you could tell me. You know I don't forget anything."

"I prefer to write it." Addi chuckled. "Nice try getting me to tell you the future though."

Chapter Eighteen

Addi divided her week between beautifying the study and hanging with Myrna. Myrna was a talker. She seemed to know quite a bit of detail about everybody in the neighborhood.

She was the opposite of Keith Jones who was a grunter. He would just silently hover around the place until Myrna told him to do something, then he would move. It was a shock to Addi when he volunteered information that he could upholster settees and offered to upholster her two broken down sofas that she had found in the music room. The material she had finally settled on matched the curtain material that Myrna sewed for her and the curtains complimented the newly painted walls.

Just like that the study/music room was becoming the most visited room in the house.

Josh and Randy had taken up residence in there since they found the Game Boys, and her mother started playing the piano again.

Her father after he came back from Negril had taken to sitting in the room in the dark. He frightened her twice.

Another week had gone down in history, and she was no closer to coming up with a plan to solving any of her family's looming problems.

Josh had taken up late night telephone chats with Ellie. Addi could hear him whispering and giggling in the hall.

Randy was acting much different than he did in the other timeline. This summer he did a lot of running. Sometimes with Josh and other times alone. He avoided her as much as possible, or was she the one avoiding him?

Her daily trips to Myrna's replaced her daily trips to the office. Tuesday of the other week had her feeling restless and edgy. Myrna wasn't overly talkative that day either. She looked as if she was contemplating something.

If Addi hadn't been so preoccupied with the state of affairs in her family, she would have noticed that Myrna wanted to say something but was hesitant.

"Mrs. Porter, your aunt, wanted me to do some drapes for her," Myrna said as an opening.

Addi nodded. She was sitting in a white plastic chair looking out into the yard. Feeling helpless and slightly hopeless. Everything was going nearly the same as the other summer of 92. Josh was still seeing Ellie, either her father or uncle was seeing Ellie too, and Uncle Stan was still on the path to be murdered by Rusty.

Myrna cleared her throat. "She er...she is a very strict lady, isn't she? I used to think she was so proper."

"Who, my aunt?" Addi asked.

"Yes," Myrna muttered, "I shouldn't say anything."

"What?" Addi straightened up and started to take notice of Myrna's hesitant speech and loaded silence.

"Well, your aunt...she's ah... she's very into Rusty, isn't

she?"

"Rusty?" Addi shook her head, "what do you mean into him?"

"Well, I passed her vehicle more than once parked near his house. I see the two of them in there talking." Myrna looked sorry that she had said it. She finished hurriedly, "but I know that she is a happily married Christian woman with very good taste in clothes, so I shouldn't have said a word."

Addi felt goose pimples spring on her arm. "Right," she said out loud.

Rusty and Ivy? No. Impossible. Rusty could be Ivy's son. She was twenty years older than he was.

She stayed just a few minutes more with Myrna and almost ran toward the office where Randy was. She flung open the office door surprising him with her entrance.

He was on the phone. She impatiently waited for him to finish.

"Yes, Miss Addison." He looked at her, his brown eyes trained on her face. "What can I do for you?"

"Aunt Ivy and Rusty," she said and sat down hard on the chair in front of the desk. "My prim and proper aunt and Sky's crush Rusty."

Randy sighed and leaned back in the chair. "Is he the lanky brown fellow that comes by sometimes for his pay?"

"Yes." Addi nodded vigorously, "he is the one. He is also the same fellow that killed my uncle over a supposed pay dispute."

"Pay dispute? And I was the one who did the payroll before?"

"Yes." Addi nodded.

"They have time cards that they punch when they go on the site. We instituted it last week to reduce any problems with pay and time worked and all of that. Besides, your father would be the person to handle pay disputes. Your uncle doesn't concern himself much with that side of the business." Randy swiped his hand over his face. "This is serious business, Addi. This is police work."

Addi snorted. "Oh yes, I can see it now. We got to the police about a murder not yet committed with no evidence that a murder will be committed except my recollections from the future."

Randy sighed. "So what are we saying here about your aunt? She is cheating on your uncle with this guy, Rusty. And then this Rusty guy kills your uncle because he is jealous or something?"

Addi nodded and then shook her head. "I don't know. Yes, no, maybe."

"We need to investigate her like we did Ellie," Addi muttered, "and then we need to warn Uncle Stan."

Randy frowned. "I do not like this 'we' business, Addi. You have Sky now; she should be your new go-to person. You are cousins, the same age; you could do your little Nancy Drew thing with her. Please don't involve me anymore."

"But I cannot do it without you, and we are talking about Sky's mother. This may be too much for her to deal with." Addi entreated him. "You have always been the one person in my life I can count on to help me with anything."

Randy looked at her and then away. "Addi I have been avoiding you."

"I noticed," Addi muttered. "I have been avoiding you too."

Randy laughed dryly. "I see glimpses of these feelings that you tell me I am going to have, and I can't be that Randy. The one from your future. The one who has this torrid affair with you while married…not going to happen. I cannot be friends with you this time around. I can't be too involved in your life."

"I know." Addi looked down at her hands and then up at him. "I understand."

The silence became so thick she could cut it with a knife.

Randy finally broke it. "You should find out from Myrna what time she spotted your aunt talking to this guy and where he lives. I can convince Josh to run in that direction when we go jogging this evening. We could check it out."

Addi nodded and got up. "Sure. Thanks, Randy."

Randy looked at her dispassionately. "After this, that's it."

"Yes." Addi nodded. "That's it."

****

Myrna reluctantly confirmed that she had seen Ivy's car near Rusty's gate three evenings at around 6:30 in the evening.

That was about two miles up the road, in the opposite direction to which Josh and Randy usually run in the evenings. Addi had no intention of sitting at home twiddling her thumbs while Josh and Randy discovered Aunt Ivy doing something that could have implications for her uncle this summer.

She got ready long before they were. Sitting in the living room with her sneakers on and her tracksuit hood pulled over her hair.

Sky saw her sitting and waiting and decided that she too would be coming along. Addi couldn't convince her otherwise, and so the four of them went jogging toward Rusty's place.

Addi and Sky could barely keep up with the men as they effortlessly ran up the street. Josh had not wanted them to come along, and he was setting a punishing pace.

At least Randy slowed down long enough for them to catch

up to him. He wasn't even panting.

"Now this is what I call slow." He laughed as both Sky and Addi were trying to catch their breaths. Addi was wheezing. She plopped herself down on a rock at the side of the road.

"My Gosh man." She looked at Randy. Her heart felt as if it were beating in her ear. "Why are you two so show off?"

Sky hung her head down and clutched her ankles. "I just remembered that I wanted to tell you something."

"What?" Addi inhaled and exhaled rapidly hoping her heart rate could come back to normal.

"I realized that some parts of the book that I wrote still has impressions on the page. You know like you can see words but not clearly."

"That's cool!" Addi exhaled on a rush.

Randy nodded. "You can shade it with a pencil to see the words."

"Yes!" Sky nodded. "I am going to do that. Shade the whole book."

"With a soft hand don't press too hard," Randy said stretching. "Do it one page at a time."

"All right." Sky chuckled. "You know I am near Colleen's house. I could stop over and wait for you guys to come back. When you said jogging, I didn't think that we would be training for the Olympics."

Addi stood up on wobbly legs. "Nah, you are coming with us."

Sky pouted. "Okay. But I think you and I should set our own pace."

Randy grinned. "I can't have you two running alone. I'll stick around."

They started walking.

Randy and Sky started on a discussion on houses and what they wanted to be included in theirs when they built it. Addi tuned them out. She had heavier thoughts on her mind. Like would they even catch aunt Ivy red-handed with her young lover?

And was he even her lover? She had no clue about this in the last timeline.

They passed Rusty's house. Sky was the one who pointed it out. It was a simple white adobe type house with lots of bougainvilleas at the front.

"Rusty lives there with his aunt and her husband and his cousins and Precious, his girlfriend." Sky sighed. "I had liked Rusty so much."

Randy glanced at Addi.

"But I am over him." Sky declared with aplomb. "First of all, he has a girlfriend, and secondly, he killed my father in some other version of this universe, and third that kiss was sub-par."

"Keep your voice down," Addi hissed.

Sky glanced at her. "There is nobody out here to hear me."

Addi looked over at the yard. It was indeed deserted, and there was no sign of Ivy's vehicle close to the road.

They walked a distance past the house and then they saw Josh stretching. "I was going to run up the hill over there." Josh pointed to a dirt track that was fairly wide.

"Had to wait on you slow coaches so that you know where I headed to."

He took off as soon as they got close to him.

Sky stood with her hands akimbo. "No way am I running, walking, or crawling up there. That's steep."

"Come on," Randy joked. "Where is your sense of adventure?"

"Gone," Sky sniffed, "about two miles ago."

Randy walked behind them and pushed them up the hill. "Now go," he said as he heralded them up the path.

They eventually started walking on their own but slowly. Randy jogged ahead of them and then slowed down for them to catch up with him. That continued for a while until they met up on Josh nearly at the top of the hill. He was sitting at the side of the road his head in his hand.

"Ha," Sky laughed. "You bit off more than you could chew didn't you, Mr. Fitness."

Josh looked up at them dazedly. "I er there is er..."

"I am going to the top," Sky said gleefully, "doesn't seem as far and because we slowly walked it up, I have the energy. Let's go, Addi. Let Josh, the hare, see that the race is not for the swift but the tortoises that endure to the end."

"No!" Josh shouted. "No!"

"Why not?" Addi was beginning to get concerned. Josh was acting off and very weird.

"Because..." Josh inhaled.

"Aunt Ivy?" She asked slowly.

Josh looked at her sharply. "Yes. How did you know?"

"I wish I could tell you time travel," Addi glanced at Sky and Randy, "but Myrna said she saw them together couple evenings ago."

Sky widened her eyes. "My mom is up there with some man?"

"Yes." Josh stretched out his legs. "This guy works for us. I think his name is Rusty. They were going at it in the car. When you think about it, this is a nice spot. It's private. It's hardly visited. I think some developer is going to make this into a nice area. The view up there is nice."

Sky sat down where she was standing in the middle of the dusty red dirt. She looked at Addi and Randy and then closed her eyes.

"Sky?" Addi asked gently. "You just said you were over Rusty."

"I know," Sky muttered. "I just can't process this..."

"Maybe we should go talk to her," Addi said, "let her know we are on to her."

"No." Randy shook his head. "We should leave."

Sky shook her head. "I don't think I can move now. I don't think that I can get up."

Randy hauled her up, and she leaned on him. All her energy was sapped. Addi hated to see her that way.

"Sky," Addi held her around the waist to the other side of Randy, and they walked down the hill with Sky propped between them like a rag doll.

She finally regained her strength after they hit the road. The tears started when they were halfway home.

It didn't let up even when they solemnly entered the yard. Sky didn't even head for her home she made a beeline straight for Addi's room.

****

It was a quiet dinner that evening. Everyone seemed preoccupied with their thoughts. Vicky declared in the middle of a prolonged silence that she was going to host Sunday dinner this week.

"You should take your girlfriend, Josh. Last Sunday you didn't take her to Ivy's. This Sunday, no disappearing on me."

Addi sighed inwardly. Her mother was going to try to outdo Aunt Ivy's previous weeks' dinner and more than likely something would go wrong. Whenever her mother tried to show off, something always went wrong.

"I thought that since the four of you went running this evening, you would all have a large appetite," Vicky looked at them.

Sky was pushing around her food morosely. Josh was

eating slowly almost absently, and Addi wasn't even pretending. She didn't want any food.

Sausage and baked beans and rice was not her dream meal. Besides, future events were weighing on her mercilessly.

She took a token bite under her mother's watchful eye and then tried to pass some over to Randy. This wasn't his family that was falling apart. He had a perfectly good appetite, and he seemed to love the dish.

After the long, tedious dinner Sky excused herself and went into the study with her blank book. Addi and Josh washed up the dishes in near silence.

Randy was on the phone with his grandma.

Josh looked at her after a while. "You can't time travel. It's fiction."

Addi nodded. "Yes, I can, I have."

Josh nodded. "Say I believe that you are a time traveler. What is it that you know about Ellie and me in the future?"

Addi felt her heart pick up speed. Was he seriously asking her? Would he believe?

"You sure you want to know?" She almost whispered the question.

"Yes." Josh exhaled. "I'll hear you out. I won't get upset."

"She gets pregnant sometime in August."

Josh swallowed.

"You two get married in December. She has a son, you named him Nelson, but he's sickly. Your blood types don't match when you volunteer to give him blood. You divorce in 96."

Josh wiped his hand on the cloth hanging by the stove and then leaned on the counter and looked at her.

"So, she is cheating on me, now?"

"Yes." Addi nodded. "With a married man. I know that now only because Randy and I went to spy on her two weeks ago. She receives money from a married man every Monday. The man who delivered the money to her asked her why she didn't leave the boss and be with him."

Addi cleared her throat.

"That man works for Porter Brothers."

Josh flinched as if he had been slapped.

"You asked for it." Addi sighed. "By the way, you get that scholarship to MIT that you applied for, and you didn't bother to take it because she had a difficult pregnancy."

Josh nodded. "Anything else?"

"If you take a different route this summer," Addi said carefully. "There is nothing I can tell you about your future. This summer is a reset point for your life."

"A married man? Dad or uncle?" Josh wiped his hand down his face. "I suspect that something is off. I wouldn't have been so suspicious if it weren't for you and your warning a while back when we were painting your room.

"You had me looking into the way we met. It was real fishy. I have always gone to Mack J's for lunch, and I've seen her, but she has never spoken to me, though she's worked there for a year.

"All of a sudden three weeks ago she is into me. I think we are moving too fast. She wants to get intimate too soon. This is not the way I operate."

He glanced at Addi. "I always do the chasing. Not to say I don't like how aggressive she is but...you spoiled it for me."

"I did?" Addi widened her eyes. "Thank God! I thought I wasn't getting through to you. I thought that history would repeat itself."

Josh shook his head. "Not for me."

"What made you suddenly decide to believe me?" Addi asked puzzled.

"I overheard you," Josh said quietly. "I overheard your

conversation with Randy this evening. All of it. You think that Uncle Stan is going to be killed. You think that Rusty did it. You were telling him that he was the only one you could rely on to believe you. I could hear the truth in your voice. I could hear it when you said that you just wanted to help your family and put things right.

"And then I got to thinking, since that day when I saw you outside with the book in your hand. I could sense that you weren't the same, your hair, clothes, room, even your cooking." Josh shook his head, "the study. You've been changing them. You talk differently. Like you are more mature. I think everybody has picked up on that. Your knowledge about my favorite artistes dying, believe it or not, was not that convincing."

Addi chuckled. "Yes, I can see why."

Then she sobered up. "What are we going to do about the Ellie issue?"

Josh winced. "Invite her to dinner. It will be our last dinner together. If she is seeing my uncle, the invitation should make her uncomfortable. She wheedled out of Aunt Ivy's invite last week. Now I know why."

"And Aunt Ivy?" Addi whispered. "What about her?"

Josh shrugged. "I don't know."

"And Uncle Stan?"

"I would prefer to kill Rusty first."

Addi sighed. "I didn't come back to save you from Ellie and then have you end up in jail."

"We will think of something." Josh patted her arm.

Chapter Nineteen

Addi was half asleep near midnight when Sky came into the room.

"Addi," she whispered loud enough to jerk Addi out of her half slumber.

"Mmmh," Addi mumbled.

Sky flipped on the side lamp. "I have a few pages!"

She was almost hopping with excitement. "There are some places where I press hard with a pen. And the outline is easy to make out. There are places where I have stuff in captions. Mainly titles. Want to hear?"

"Of course." Addi made room for Sky on the bed. "Didn't you go home?"

"No," Sky muttered. "Told the cheating witch that I was sleeping over here."

"Sky, you can't go calling your mother a cheating witch."

"Yeah, right." Sky snorted. "Listen to this:

Hi Sky,

I know that this will be shocking to you if Addi makes it back with this book and you are reading this. If you are reading this and it is July 1992. You owe Addison Porter your life. She is the best person in the entire world.

So without further ado, let me tell you. Your future life sucks. You live in a huge modern apartment in Manhattan. You are the boss of a large corporation. People scurry to do your bidding. You are Miss Bitch, but you are so unhappy. And you can't take it anymore. Why the deep unhappiness?

Well, there was Rusty, in the summer of 92, July 25th to be exact, you had sex with him on a hillside in the middle of nowhere. Don't do it. For the love of Jesus, don't do it. He is not worth it.

He is a user. You are not in love. You are a crazy teenager under the influence of some serious chemical imbalances.

That brings me to this— he killed Dad. Pushed him off the second story of the apartment of a site he is working on. The date August 15th, two weeks after you've had sex with the slime. That is what he has used to tie you to him for all these years and made you feel guilty about your own father's death,

His reason for the incident is that he told Dad that he wanted to date you and they had a fight, and he pushed him.

That's why you supported him through the years, visited him in prison and took care of the child he fathered with Precious. In general, it is the reason you carried Rusty's burden for your whole life because you thought it was your fault that your father died.

Sky stopped reading.

Addi looked at her. "Go on."

"I had sex with him?" Sky grimaced, "in the same spot he did it with my mother? Can you say massively gross?"

"Just read the thing," Addi said impatiently.

Sky looked back down on the pages.

Well, you had no reason to be carrying that stupid burden all of these years. Rusty is not worth it. He was having an affair with Ivy Porter who I will not dare call my mother anymore.

She paid Rusty fifteen thousand dollars to get rid of Dad. Yes, that's right. She paid that rotten piece of filth, money to kill your father and then had the nerve to cry at his funeral. Every year she put a flower on his headstone, like a true grieving widow.

But Rusty told you all of this a week ago. He finally came clean on the day that he was released from prison. He has served his time. You have served yours. You have been wracked with guilt for all these years. You have allowed that event in 92 to rule your life. Trust me, Sky, you have never had a happy day since. If Addi managed to go back before any of this happened. Please, stop it. Do not let any of this happen.

Sky folded the book close to her after closing it.

"Anything else?" Addi asked, her voice trembling. She felt a cold, shivering sensation when she thought about it.

Her aunt Ivy had paid Rusty to kill Uncle Stan?

"Yeah." Sky muttered, "She...well me...there are some stock tips and share prices and a long list of don't do this, don't do that, sort of thing. There is a piece in there titled Addi."

"Me?" Addi squealed. "You shaded it yet?"

"Yes." Sky handed her the book.

Addi took it and read.

Tell Addi, that I know about her lifelong affair with Randy. Tell her she needs to make the most of this time with him again. Tell her that light blue is a beautiful color on her.

Tell her that this time around she should explore her

artistic side. Tell her to live a little and to stop overthinking things. Tell her to stop and smell the roses. The nineties were our good old days before the beginning of the technological explosion before we got too busy for people.

Tell her, don't lose touch with Julia and Annette, they were good—solid friends.

The following stocks and shares for her to invest in and build a healthy portfolio. If she is going to live her life again, no rule says that this time she shouldn't do it comfortably. The stocks are attached.

Addi laughed. "Only you."

Sky took back the book and looked thoughtful.

"My mom paid Rusty to kill my dad?"

"She hasn't done it yet," Addi said determinedly. "And she is not going to get a chance to do it. Let's get some sleep."

Sky eased herself under the sheet and turned off the lamplight.

"Thank God, you haven't had sex with Rusty," Addi muttered. "Now go to sleep."

"I will never," Sky whispered in the dark. "Especially not after today. Thanks for resetting me, Addi."

"You are welcome," Addi mumbled as sleep threatened to overtake her again.

"Tell me about you and Randy," Sky whispered when the fringes of sleep were on the verge of taking over.

Addi just grunted. "There is no me and Randy."

****

Vicky was in full hostess mode on Sunday. The competition was on. Addi could see from the set table that it wasn't going to be an ordinary competition either; her mother had set the table with her best China. The smells from the kitchen were too scrumptious for words.

Everybody was still in their Sunday best, sitting around as Vicky flitted in and out of the kitchen and gave them staccato orders.

"You, bring me some thyme." She pointed at Sky.

Sky got up hurriedly and went toward the thyme bush at the side of the house.

"You," she pointed at Addi, "have you set the table for Ellie?"

"Yes, Mom." Addi nodded. Josh had gone to pick up Ellie. Randy and her father and uncle were watching English premier league football.

Her dad and uncle were quite oblivious to the dinner preparations. They were so caught up in the game that it would probably take lightning to rouse them from the game.

Addi looked at the two of them and shook her head. For the past couple of days, they had mini-meetings in the study to discuss the way forward—to plot strategy.

They hadn't agreed on what to do yet. Whatever they did the family would be in trouble. Nobody wanted that to happen. But everybody agreed that today had to be significant.

Whatever happened, it would not end up being a fairytale. Not one bit.

Aunt Ivy came over soon after Sky returned with the thyme.

She sat on the settee gingerly and looked around, a look of distaste on her face and then her eyes settled on the framed calendars.

"I like these pictures," She finally said.

Addi nodded. She forced herself to assess Aunt Ivy. She looked so innocent. Her hair was combed back in her favorite bun style. Her eyebrows plucked a little bit too high, her mouth thin, her eyes darted around the room as she reluctantly admired Vicky's pictures.

Why set up someone to kill her husband though?

Why not just leave him?

Now Addi knew why Ivy had avoided them at all cost in the future. Why she had locked herself away for months after. She was ashamed to face them knowing what she had done.

It was ironic how time and knowledge had thrown her aunt's behavior in a different light.

"So, Addi, do you know why my daughter is avoiding me like the plague?"

Addi jumped, she had been so deep in thought. She looked at Sky who was hovering around the kitchen area and then shook her head.

"She was avoiding me the other day too. Sky is just weird."

"I'd say." Ivy looked over at Sky. "Honey, come here and sit down."

Sky shook her head. "No, er thanks. I am going to help Aunt Vicky take the food to the table."

Ivy sighed. "Very well. So, Nate, how are you? Maybe I should ask my husband the same question too. I hardly speak to either one of you these days. I feel as if I live on another planet."

"I am good Ivy." Her father reluctantly dragged his eyes from the television. "Work. Busy."

Ivy snorted in disgust.

Uncle Stan didn't look at her. He continued watching television as if she had not spoken.

Ivy sighed loudly. "Football is the mistress."

Neither brother reacted.

"Maybe I should go and give a helping hand to Victoria. I know how she always mangles the sauce."

"No thanks," Vicky called from the kitchen. "I will soon be out. I didn't do anything fancy…just fried fish, curried goat, jerk chicken and some baked mac and cheese and sweet potato salad and of course potato wedges, white rice and tossed salad. Of course, I also did bread pudding and ice cream."

"Good lord," her father muttered, he glanced over at Addi and grinned.

Addi moved her face into the semblance of a smile. Nobody in this house was going to be smiling for much longer.

Josh arrived with Ellie after her mother came to the doorway and announced that dinner would be ready in five minutes.

Ellie's arrival was anticlimactic.

Both her father and uncle greeted her absently. There was no special and lingering look. No indication of which one of them had an affair with her.

Ellie sat beside Addi and was engrossed in the sport just like the men, offering offhand comments and acting like one of the guys.

Ivy was obviously poised for a conversation with her but was shut out.

Josh absented himself to his room for a while. Randy who was looking at the Sunday Gleaner with interest was the first one to jump up when dinner was announced.

Addi didn't think she imagined it, but the air was thick with tension.

The food was good. Her mother had outdone herself. After the grace and the general chitchat, everyone at the table became solemn.

"Why is everybody so somber?" Vicky looked around the table. "It can't be the food. Is it?"

"No. Mrs. Porter this is very good." Randy was the first to speak.

"Very." Ellie was tucking into her plate like a starving

Judas.

Ivy cleared her throat. "Well, the food is acceptable. I am not sure why everyone is so solemn, but I know I would be if I were you Victoria. Your son's slut girlfriend is sleeping with your husband!"

Chapter Twenty

So it was her dad. Addi wiped her mouth with the napkin. A shaft of disappointment hit her out of nowhere. She had hoped otherwise. The bombshell coming from Ivy was not unexpected, but it still hurt.

She looked around the table. Everyone was frozen as if somebody had told them to do a mannequin challenge.

Her mother was the first to move. She slowly and deliberately wiped her mouth. And then turned to Ivy.

"Repeat."

Ivy shrugged. "You heard. Nathan is sleeping with Ellie. They have a special motel, one of those sleaze places that they frequent. Saw them with my own eyes a few months ago."

Ellie was moving jerkily. She pushed away her chair. She didn't know where to look. Josh showed no reaction. He was just sitting there and shaking his head.

"I er I should go." Ellie's voice trembled.

"No," Vicky got up, "sit back down!" She glared at her husband. "Tell Ivy she is a liar, Nathan Porter!"

Addi watched as her father retreated in guilty silence. He knew to be afraid when her mother used his full name.

"She is our son's girlfriend!" Vicky yelled. She looked at both Addi and Sky. "Go to your room!"

"Ahm, no." Addi was the first one to speak. "I think what you should ask Aunt Ivy is how she knows where dad meets Ellie. Maybe, you should ask her if she was at the same place with say, maybe Rusty?"

"What?" It was Uncle Stan's turn to bellow.

Aunt Ivy subsided in her chair. "That's nonsense. Rusty is a mere uneducated construction worker. I am a school principal."

"They also meet in the hills near the new development." Sky joined in, "we all saw her with him when we went walking couple evenings ago. We caught her having sex with him."

Ivy gasped and clutched her throat like an outraged Victorian maiden.

Uncle Stan flung himself away from the table, knocking over the chair. He looked like he was going to blow. His face was red. The blood vessels at the side of his head looked enlarged.

"She is going to pay him fifteen thousand dollars to kill you, Daddy!" Sky blurted out.

All eyes were trained on Ivy who was looking back at them her eyes wide open in guilt.

She might not have done it yet, but she had thought about it. Addi inhaled shakily. She had thought about it. It was written all over her face.

Ivy didn't refute the latest accusation. She got up slowly and deliberately.

"This is preposterous. Skyler Porter, I am disappointed in you accusing your mother of something so despicable."

She said it with little heat. Her voice was breathless and guilt-riddled.

Nobody was buying that token protestation.

"Rusty is supposed to push you off the second floor of the building in Ingleside!" Sky shouted it. "Don't let Rusty back on that site Daddy and Uncle Nate!"

Sky was almost hopping with the information.

She got up. "If anything happens to my dad in the next couple of years," Sky yelled at her mother's retreating back. "If any accident, if any poison if anything happens to him even if you are not remotely near. I am blaming you! We all know what you are capable of! We all know you now Ivy!"

Ivy didn't look back at them. She walked through the door her head held high.

Stan looked at them and then at Ivy undecided whether he should follow her. "How?" He rubbed his hand over his face. "Why? Good Lord! Is any of this true?"

Sky started to sob. "Yes, Daddy. Please don't let her kill you, Daddy."

Uncle Stan had his hand full with a sobbing Sky. Days of pent-up emotions flowed freely, and she was sobbing like a heartbroken child.

Vicky was sitting with her mouth opened. She had forgotten that she had been mad at her husband.

"You must admit," Josh said after a heavy silence, "that murder is worse than an affair."

Her father lowered his eyes. "I am sorry."

"How long, Nate?" Vicky asked hoarsely. "How long has this been going on?"

"A couple of months." Nate fidgeted with his napkin. "I met her before Josh. I didn't mean for this to get so out of hand."

Ellie cleared her throat. "I should go."

"I'll drop her home," Randy said getting up. "Where are your car keys, Josh?"

"Over there." Josh hooked his thumb over his shoulders.

Addi got up too. "I'll come with you." Nobody paid attention to her.

"Wait," Vicky, said sounding militant. "I don't want you near my house again, Ellie. You hear me?"

"Yes," Ellie was shaking like a leaf. "I hear you. I won't...I am sorry."

"This is sick!" Vicky got up and headed to her room. "You are a bunch of sick people!"

****

Ellie sat in the back of the car. She was crying quietly. Now and then, they heard a hiccup.

Addi felt ridiculously relieved at the outcome.

She glanced at Randy his jaws were firmly clenched.

"Listen," Addi turned to the back of the vehicle where Ellie was slumped like a forlorn sack of rice. "You made a mistake."

Ellie looked at her, eyes red, nose runny.

"You'll learn from it," Addi said, "It could be worse. Imagine if you had gotten pregnant for my dad and then had to pawn off the child to Josh."

Ellie hiccupped.

Addi handed her a roll of paper towel that she knew Josh always had in his glove compartment.

"I am pregnant," Ellie said after a long silence.

"What?" Addi swung her head around so fast she almost got whiplash.

"I...I..." Ellie hiccupped again, "I was seeing Stan too. I haven't slept with Nathan for so long, so I know it's Stan's. And Josh has been holding out on me."

Randy stopped and looked back at Ellie, his mouth agape.

When he finally spoke, his voice was heavy with disbelief. "You were seeing the brothers and Josh. The whole family?"

"Yes." Ellie shrugged. "I only recently started with Stan. I met him when he came to the school to drop off something for Ivy. At first, I had no idea he was Nate's brother, but he was lonely, kind of like me and he is a generous man.

"He gives me money every Monday. My uncle refuses to take care of my brother. I had to do something to supplement the income for his upbringing. I was going to find a place and move with him. Your uncle promised that he would take care of that for me."

"That's why aunt Ivy had him killed," Addi whispered hoarsely. "That's why—not the Rusty thing. It was this. She must have found out and cracked."

"What are you talking about?" Ellie sniffed.

"Nothing," Addi muttered. "This summer of 92 is shaping up to be crazy as hell."

****

They dropped off Ellie.

Randy looked at the gas gauge. "Want us to drive around before we return to bedlam?"

"Yes." Addi nodded.

"In the other timeline you said she never named the father of her child," Randy said after a while. "Maybe because he was dead, and she needed the help."

"Yes." Addi nodded, "I can't believe she was sleeping with all the Porter men. If grandfather was alive, he would probably get some of the action."

Randy laughed. "The Porter men like their Ellie."

"Yep." Addi nodded.

"What do you think your mother is going to do now?" Randy asked. "Will they stay together?"

"I don't know." Addi shook her head, "I don't know."

"And Ivy? What's going to happen to her?" Randy frowned and then looked at her a smile on his face. "Why am I asking you? You have no idea, do you?"

"Nope." Addi grinned, "The rest of the summer is unchartered waters."

Randy nodded. "And you and me? Any idea?"

"We will never cheat on our spouses whoever they are." Addi smiled at him. "We see firsthand how destructive the whole unfaithfulness thing can be. Maybe if we had gone through this before...we wouldn't have happened, no way."

Randy smiled back. "Suppose my spouse turns out to be Addison Porter?"

Addi laughed. "Not likely."

Randy stopped the car and turned to her.

"If I loved you so much before. I may love you that much again. This time, I'll wait for you. Addi."

Addi gasped. "Randy, don't make me any promises. You haven't lived your life yet. You haven't yet met the girl you got married to. No promises, okay. I won't be making you any."

"Okay." Randy shrugged. "Just one. I want you to promise me that we won't lose touch with each other."

Addi sighed.

"Promise." Randy insisted.

"Okay, I promise." Addi smiled and rolled down the window.

****

December 1992

Addi started forgetting the other timeline. Trying to recall specific details was getting harder and harder. That life felt more and more like a fantasy, something she had dreamed up. Sometimes she could fuzzily recall details, but at other times she was just working with what felt like fragments of dreams.

Sometimes she heard things on television. Saw a piece of news clip and it felt familiar like she had heard it before but that feeling was becoming rarer.

Sky had been urging her for the past couple of months to write down her thoughts. She should have listened because now it was becoming harder to recall anything from the future.

She stood in Josh's room doorway and watched him pack for MIT. He was going to the States. She hadn't seen him much for the past four months since he had gone back to school. He plopped one clothes item after another into his open suitcase.

"Don't look so forlorn." Josh grinned at her, "I'll call."

"I know," Addi said sadly. "It won't be the same here without you though."

"Nothing is the same here these days." Josh sighed, "Dad keeps apologizing, Mom is a wreck, but I guess some things had to come out huh?"

"Yes." Addi nodded.

The family dynamics had changed somewhat, but her father and mother were still together, though their relationship was still frosty.

Uncle Stan had started divorce proceedings against Ivy. Stan and Sky were practically living by Addi's house now. They had most of their meals here. Sky was considering moving into Josh's room when he left.

Ivy was living in an apartment in the town area and still seeing Rusty. Rusty's girlfriend, Precious, had accosted Ivy on the job with a knife. It made the tabloid headlines for weeks: Baby Father Drama. Pregnant Woman Attacks Principal Over Man. The story had been fodder for gossip and didn't seem as if it was letting up.

Ellie had moved on with Ray. She and her brother lived with him, and she was driving around town in his vehicle happy as can be. She wasn't pregnant now. Addi supposed she lost the child or had an abortion.

Addi never told anyone what Ellie told her in the summer about being pregnant for Uncle Stan. She and Randy kept that a secret. That was one more issue her family could do without.

And Randy, he had sent her a Christmas card, and she felt ridiculously pleased to get it.

She moved away from Josh's door and headed to the hallway. Her dad and uncle were reading the Sunday paper and watching cricket on the television. Still together like peas in a pod. She imagined that they would grow old together keeping each other's secrets. She was not in any doubt that they had both known about each other's indiscretions with Ellie.

"Say Addi." Her uncle lowered the paper; it was the sports section, with the headline, West Indies On the Run.

"What do you think about the Windies chances for the rest of their series against Australia?"

Addi thought for a moment. There was nothing there. No recollections. Nothing.

"I don't know."

Her father looked over at her and smiled. "That's my girl. No more gambling with Stan."

"He is just jealous because he didn't believe you about the Summer Olympics and I made a ton of money on your suggestions." Uncle Stan wrinkled his brows. "Come on Addi, help me. You are a time traveler you should know these things."

"But the longer I am here in this timeline, the more I forget." Addi shrugged. "Sorry Uncle Stan."

Stan snorted. "So what's the use of having the super power if you have it for a limited time?"

Her father guffawed.

Addi shrugged and sat on the settee beside her dad, reaching for the magazine section of the newspaper.

"Maybe I came back to save your life."

Stan grunted. "There is that. Thanks, I guess."

"You are welcome." Addi beamed opening her paper. "It was no trouble. No trouble at all."

The End

Author's Notes

Dear Reader,

If you look into your palms and have a distinct T, please note that you have the potential to time travel. You need to find a pathway! Well, at least, that's what is happening in the resetters series. I will be making this a four-book series. So far, I am having a ball with this time traveling business. Who would have thought that the 90's would feel like the good old days? There are so many things from that era that I had forgotten about--writing this book, really felt like time traveling.

I would personally love to be a resetter. The things I would do! The things I would change! But alas, my palms have more lines than most persons. Maybe that is a thing. :)

Anyway, dear reader, I continue to live through my time traveling characters vicariously. There are three books to follow Never Too Late.

There is: Never Say Never, Sky's story. An excerpt is on th e next page.

After that, I will release Now or Never, Addi and Randy's story. Almost Never, Josh's story will close the series.

As usual, thank you for reading.

Thanks again. All the best,

Brenda

Here is an Excerpt From
Never Say Never

Summer 2000

"Skyler Porter, is it?" Mrs. Beckett, the human resource director, looked over her glasses at Sky and then down at the resume in her hand before Sky could answer.

"You have an MBA from Harvard?" The lady looked up at her again. "How old are you?"

Sky resisted the urge to roll her eyes and point out that her age was at the top of the document.

"Twenty-two," she replied in a well-modified tone.

She needed this job—if she had to suffer through obvious questions, she would suffer through them. She had no idea why Jefferson Pharmaceuticals called her at the time they did even though she had not applied for the job. Nevertheless, it was an answer to prayers because she was at a crossroad in her life.

She had the option of staying in the States with her cousin, Addi, and find a job in New York, or return to Jamaica. The decision had been made for her with an invite to a job interview.

"How did you do it?" Mrs. Beckett leaned back in her chair.

"Do what?" Sky thought that she had missed something.

"Finished your undergraduate degree by twenty and your MBA by twenty-two?"

"I just worked hard," Sky said. "I did more courses than the usual in my undergraduate studies and graduated with a perfect GPA and then went to Harvard Business School on a scholarship."

Mrs. Beckett smiled. "I am impressed."

"Thank you." Sky nodded. She was now warming up to the stern looking woman.

"As you know this is a family-owned company. Travis Jefferson is the current president of this company. His father, Manuel, started out selling cough syrup. Since the eighties, the business has grown exponentially.

"We are the leading pharmaceutical company in the Caribbean. We are a large company, and we continue to expand every day. This position of Business Development Manager is a senior management position, Miss Porter.

"Unfortunately, you have no experience whatsoever. You have a very nice degree, no doubt, but I am afraid that I can't in all good conscience recommend you for this position..."

Sky couldn't believe what she was hearing. She had not applied for this position. She had not even heard about it until she was asked to send in her resume. And now, after scraping together her airfare and spending her last dollar on an expensive suit, she was told this madness. Now, she would have to report the bad news to her father who had so exuberantly greeted her at the airport.

He had been excited at the possibilities of her living back home and closer to him. She was going to have to burst his bubble.

Sky got up slowly, disappointment ricocheting through her like fireworks.

Did this lady think that she had just been hanging out in Kingston? Did she have any idea how far she was coming from to be having this failed interview?

They could have done this over the phone!

"I am sorry Miss Porter." Mrs. Beckett held out her hand to be shaken.

She didn't look sorry.

Sky looked at her outstretched arm and for a split second

considered being rude, but she didn't. She shook the lady's hand and searched for something to say that was pleasant, something that didn't scream her disappointment.

The door to the office was unceremoniously opened before she could formulate a word and a rather handsome guy pushed his head around the door.

"Oh good, she is here. Send her to my office Bertha, will you?"

Sky frowned and looked from Mrs. Beckett to the mysterious gentleman.

Mrs. Beckett looked miffed. "But I already checked her resume as you asked me to, sir, and I think..."

He came into the room fully. He was tall—over six feet. He had dark nutmeg brown skin and jet-black wavy hair, which was brushing his collar—some of it was falling in his chocolate brown eyes. He was the definition of tall, dark and handsome.

He pushed his hand into his suit pocket and looked at Sky for longer than was polite and then back at Mrs. Beckett.

"This interview was supposed to be a formality, Bertha. If I didn't have that meeting, I would have been around to welcome Sky into the Jefferson Pharmaceutical family."

And then his magnetic brown eyes were eating her up. "I am sorry for the misunderstanding, Skyler." He moved from the doorway and advanced to her with a smile in his eyes.

"My name is Travis Jefferson. Will you be so kind as to walk with me to my office?"

Sky nodded as if she was in a daze. He called her Sky with a hint of familiarity that was puzzling and exciting at the same time.

This was the Travis Jefferson, the head of the company. She had no idea he was so young, maybe early thirties and no idea that he was so attractive. Sky tried not to stare when she walked closer to him. She could smell his cologne—something earthy.

She had the insane urge to stop and sniff him. Instead, she concentrated on looking professional and followed him to the bank of elevators. His office was three floors up from where she met Mrs. Beckett.

He stood apart from her in the elevator and stared at her as if he wanted to say something.

Sky felt a bit self-conscious. She suffered through his silent regard and then followed him through the carpeted hallway and into his office.

Up here in the hallowed hallways of richness was obviously where the executives resided. Every door had a name embossed in brass, each of which had a VP of whatever on it.

His door was wider than the rest. There was a sub-office before another door. A lady who Sky assumed was his secretary was sitting at a desk. She was on the telephone.

"Hold my calls, Betty, and no visitors," Travis said before they headed to another door, which Sky assumed was his office.

The office was large and tastefully done. One section of the wall was made of stone, with little niches in the wall, which were filled with flowerpots with bright looking plants—each blooming a different color.

A small conference table was at one end and in the middle was his desk. There was a patio filled with plants and a view of the mountains in the distance.

"Nice." Sky looked around. "This is a dream office."

Travis indicated for her to sit in a seat across from him and then he leaned over the desk smiling. "I have been keeping track of your educational pursuits, Miss Porter."

"You have?" Sky was trying not to act surprised.

But he could see that she was.

He scratched his head and then laughed. "My God, it's going to take time explaining this to you."

"What are you going on about?" Sky asked frowning. "Do you know me from somewhere?"

He smiled. "I believe I do, Miss Porter. Not from some other place but some other time."

Fire and Walter (Book 3)- Walter's past came rushing to greet him shortly after his appointment as church elder. The new pastor was his childhood molestor, his wife was his ex from college and her cousin was the girl who got away. Walter had a lot of decisions to make.

The Perfect Guy (Book 4) - After a patient five years waiting for Lucia, Guy had his work cut out for him to prove himself worthy of her affections. He had played the part of poor farmer for too long and now he had competition in the form of the handsome doctor Ace Jackson.

The Patience of A Saint (Book 5)- Something was wrong with Saint's wife Sandrene. It didn't take a genius to see that she was changed beyond all recognition. Saint had to get to the bottom of it, before it was too late for them to salvage anything from the relationship.

A Case of Love (Book 6)- After a concert, Case is offered a girl to buy. Her fate was in his hands. He could keep her or leave her to the mercy of her evil family.

Resetter Series

Never Too Late (Book 1)- Addi finds out she is a resetter and goes back to the summer of 92 to change her family's lives.

Never Say Never (Book 2)- Skyler's handsome college lecturer, who happens to be her neighbor, has a 't' in his palms. Should she tell him the significance of it. If she does, would he believe her?

Now or Never (Book 3)- Ten years later Addi and Randy meet again at Randy's engagement party. Why is it that the chemistry between them was still so potent? Can they ever have a future together? Would Randy choose her this time around?

Almost Never (Book 4)- Tech genius Joshua Porter had all but given up on love. He then meets Portia, an inmate at the female penitentiary and his life takes a turn for the adventurous.

The Scarlett Family Series

Scarlett Baby (Book 1)- When the head of the Scarlett family died, Yuri had to return home to Treasure Beach for the funeral. What he didn't count on was seeing Marla, his childhood sweetheart and his best friend's wife. And when emotions overwhelm them and a few months later Marla is pregnant, Yuri wants the impossible: his best friend's wife and the baby they made together...

Scarlett Sinner (Book 2)- Pastor Troy Scarlett realizes the hard way that some sins are bound to be revealed, like the child that he had out of wedlock with his wife's mortal enemy from college. His wife Chelsea was not happy with the status quo. She was not taking care of the son of the woman she had so despised from college. And she could not get over the deep betrayal that she felt from her husband's indiscretion.

Scarlett Secret (Book 3)- Terri Scarlett had a soft spot for her friend, Lola. She was funny and sweet and they looked remarkably alike. But when Lola's Arab prince demands his bride, Terri foolishly exchange places with her friend and they meet up on a world of trouble.

Scarlett Love (Book 4)- Slater always looked forward to delivering packages to the law firm where he could get a glimpse of the stunning female lawyer, Amoy Gardener. Unfortunately, for Slater a woman like Amoy would not take him seriously, especially when she found out that he could not read!

Scarlett Promise (Book 5)- Driven by desperation Lisa Barclay decides to make some extra money by prostituting herself after being kicked out in the streets. Her first customer turns out to be a popular government senator and then to her horror he dies...

Scarlett Bride (Book 6)- When Oliver Scarlett's missionary work in the Congo region was coming to an end, he had a decision to make, marry Ashaki Azanga and save her from being the fourth wife to the chief of the village or leave her to her fate and get on with his life...

Scarlett Heart (Book 7)- After receiving a heart transplant shy librarian Noah Scarlett started to take on character traits that were unlike him and he kept dreaming of a girl named Cassandra Green...

Rebound Series

On The Rebound- For Better or Worse, Brandon vowed to stay with Ashley, but when worse got too much he moved out and met Nadine. For the first time in years he felt happy, but then Ashley remembered her wedding vows...

On The Rebound 2- Ashley reinvented herself and was

now a first lady in a country church in Primrose Hill, but her obsessed ex friend Regina showed up and started digging into the lives of the saints at church. Somebody didn't like Regina's digging. Someone had secrets that were shocking enough to kill for...

Magnolia Sisters

Dear Mystery Guy (Book 1)- Della Gold details her life in a journal dedicated to a mystery guy. But when fascination turns into obsession she finds herself wanting to learn even more about him but in her pursuit of the mystery guy she begins to learn more about herself...

Bad Girl Blues (Book 2)- Brigid Manderson wanted to go to med school but for the time being she was an escort working for her mother, an ex-prostitute. When her latest customer offers her the opportunity of a lifetime would she take it? Or would she choose the harder path and uncertain love with a Christian guy?

Her Mistaken Dreams (Book 3)- Caitlin Denvers dream guy had serious issues. He has a dead wife in his past and he was the main suspect in her murder. Did he really do it? Or did Caitlin for the first time have a mistaken dream?

Just Like Yesterday (Book 4)- Hazel Brown lost six months of memory including the summer that she conceived her son, and had no idea who his father could be. Now that she had the means to fight to get him back from the Deckers, she finds out that the handsome Curtis Decker is willing to share her son with her after all.

New Song Series

Going Solo (Book 1)- Carson Bell, had a lovely voice, a heart of gold, and was no slouch in the looks department. So why did Alice abandon him and their daughter? What did she want after ten years of silence?

Duet on Fire (Book 2)- Ian and Ruby had problems trying to conceive a child. If that wasn't enough, her ex-lover the current pastor of their church wants her back...

Tangled Chords (Book 3)- Xavier Bell, the poor, ugly duckling has made it rich and his looks have been incredibly improved too. Farrah Knight, hotel heiress had cruelly rejected him in the past but now she needed help. Could Xavier forgive and forget?

Broken Harmony(Book 4)- Aaron Lee, wanted the top job in his family company but he had a moral clause to consider just when Alka, his married ex-girlfriend walks back into his life.

A Past Refrain (Book 5)- Jayce had issues with forgetting Haley Greenwald even though he had a new woman in his life. Will he ever be able to shake his love for Haley?

Perfect Melody (Book 6)- Logan Moore had the perfect wife, Melody but his secretary Sabrina was hell bent on breaking up the family. Sabrina wanted Logan whatever the cost and she had a secret about Melody, that could shatter Melody's image to everyone.

The Bancroft Family Series

Homely Girl (Book 0) - April and Taj were opposites in so many ways. He was the cute, athletic boy that everybody wanted to be friends with. She was the overweight, shy, and withdrawn girl. Do April and Taj have a love that can last a lifetime? Or will time and separate paths rip them apart?

Saving Face (Book 1) - Mount Faith University drama begins with a dead president and several suspects including the president in waiting Ryan Bancroft.

Tattered Tiara (Book 2) - Micah Bancroft is targeted by femme fatale Deidra Durkheim. There are also several rape cases to be solved.

Private Dancer (Book 3) Adrian Bancroft was gutted when he returned to Jamaica and found out that his first and only love Cathy Taylor was a stripper and was literally owned by the menacing drug lord, Nanjo Jones.

Goodbye Lonely (Book 4) - Kylie Bancroft was shy and had to resort to going to confidence classes. How could she win the love of Gareth Beecher, her faculty adviser, a man with a jealous ex-wife in his past and a current mystery surrounding a hand found in his garden?

Practice Run (Book 5) - Marcus Bancroft had many reasons to avoid Mount Faith but Deidra Durkheim was not one of them. Unfortunately, on one of his visits he was the victim of a deliberate hit and run.

Sense of Rumor (Book 6) - Arnella Bancroft was the wild, passionate Bancroft, the creative loner who didn't mind living dangerously; but when a terrible thing happened to her at her friend Tracy's party, it changed her. She found that courting rumors can be devastating and that only the truth could set her free.

A Younger Man (Book 7)- Pastor Vanley Bancroft loved Anita Parkinson despite their fifteen-year age gap, but Anita had a secret, one that she could not reveal to Vanley. To tell him would change his feelings toward her, or force him to give up the ministry that he loved so much.

Just To See Her (Book 8)- Jessica Bancroft had the opportunity to meet her fantasy guy Khaled, he was finally coming to Mount Faith but she had feelings for Clay Reid, a guy who had all the qualities she was looking for. Who would she choose and what about the weird fascination Khaled had for Clay?

The Three Rivers Series

Private Sins (Book 1)- Kelly, the first lady at Three Rivers Church was pregnant for the first elder of her church. Could she keep the secret from her husband and pretend that all was well?

Loving Mr. Wright (Book 2)- Erica saw one last opportunity to ditch her single life when Caleb Wright appeared in her town. He was perfect for her, but what was he hiding?

Unholy Matrimony (Book 3) - Phoebe had a problem, she was poor and unhappy. Her solution to marry a rich man was derailed along the way with her feelings for Charles Black, the poor guy next door.

If It Ain't Broke (Book 4)- Chris Donahue wanted a place in his child's life. Pinky Black just wanted his love. She also wanted him to forget his obsession with Kelly and love her. That shouldn't be so hard? Should it?

Contemporary Romance/Drama

After The End--Torn between two lovers. Colleen married her high school sweetheart, Isaiah, hoping that they would live happily ever after but life intruded and Isaiah disappeared at sea. She found work with the rich and handsome, Enrique Lopez, as a housekeeper and realized that she couldn't keep him at arms length...

Love Triangle: Three Sides To The Story- George, the husband, Marie, the wife and Karen-the mistress. They all get to tell their side of the story.

The Preacher And The Prostitute - Prostitution and the clergy don't mix. Tell that to ex-prostitute, Maribel, who finds herself in love with the Pastor at her church. Can an ex-prostitute and a pastor have a future together?

New Beginnings - Inner city girl Geneva was offered an opportunity of a lifetime when she found out that her 'real' father was a very wealthy man. Her decision to live up-town meant that she had to leave Froggie, her 'ghetto don,' behind. She also found herself battling with her stepmother and battling her emotions for Justin, a suave up-towner.

Full Circle- After graduating from university, Diana wanted to return to Jamaica to find her siblings. What she didn't foresee was that she would meet Robert Cassidy and that both their pasts would be intertwined, and that disturbing questions would pop up about their parentage, just when they were getting close.

Historical Fiction/Romance

The Empty Hammock- Workaholic, Ana Mendez, fell asleep in a hammock and woke up in the year 1494. It was the time of the Tainos, a time when life seemed simpler, but Ana knew that all of that was about to change.

The Pull Of Freedom- Even in bondage the people, freshly arrived from Africa, considered themselves free. Led by Nanny and Cudjoe the slaves escaped the Simmonds' plantation and went in different directions to forge their destiny in the new country called Jamaica.

Jamaican Comedy (Material contains Jamaican dialect)

Di Taxi Ride And Other Stories- Di Taxi Ride and Other Stories is a collection of twelve witty and fast paced short stories. Each story tells of a unique slice of Jamaican life.

www.ingramcontent.com/pod-product-compliance
Lightning Source LLC
Chambersburg PA
CBHW02094718 0626
46814CB00003B/977